To Nicky

Thank you for beig a great fan.

Happy Reading

CM Denning

WHAT HE NEEDS

Other books by E. M. Denning:

Bright Lights
Boomerang
Revenge
Little Love on the Prairie
Measure For Measure
Alpha Tango
At The Barre
Jazz Hands
Break
The Forbidden Dance

E.M. DENNING

First Paper Gold Publishing paperback edition January 2018

Printed and bound in the United States of America

For Shaw

1
Craig

HE SHOULDN'T BE NERVOUS. He'd done it before. He'd walked into clubs before and never felt the sickening swirl of his stomach as its contents prepared for launch. Craig swallowed, then popped another antacid into his mouth and chewed it up.

He could do this. He needed to do this. He normally hated the club atmosphere, but it had pleased Tim to take him places and show him off, and if he hoped to move on he needed this. He had needed to get over Tim. He needed someone who would give him the things Tim gave him and there was only one kind of place where you were guaranteed to meet the kind of person Craig needed to meet. Tails had a reputation as a popular kink club. Tim had never taken him to this club, and Craig hoped that he'd be able to go in there. He'd tried to visit a different club a few weeks ago, but couldn't make it past the bouncer.

It was a place he'd frequented with Tim and the bouncer recognized him on sight. He looked at him with those big, sympathetic brown eyes and Craig's insides liquefied. He quickly lost his nerve and hurried back the way he came. Everyone understood what happened to him, well, everyone in that circle knew. It was why he hadn't talked to any of his former kink friends since Tim left him. Maybe if he did, he could at least figure out what he did to drive Tim away. Perhaps he could find out why he came home from work one day to find all of Tim's stuff gone.

Craig cursed himself and wiped away an errant tear. He needed someone to get him out of his head before he lost his mind completely. Tim had been perfect for him. Roommates at first, then friends, then lovers. One fateful night they stumbled into something more; something that took everything they had together and made it all that much better and more powerful and meaningful. Or so Craig thought.

They spent a year together exploring the lifestyle. Both newbies, they muddled through a little on their own before Tim insisted they join a club and do it right. Everything seemed perfect. Tim was a good Dom. Sure, he made a few newbie mistakes, but Craig made some mistakes as a first time sub. Despite the times they stumbled, discovering his need for submission had to be the best thing that ever happened to Craig. Even when Tim wanted things that Craig didn't feel comfortable with, he still relished belonging to him. Craig figured that even though they were out of sync to begin with that over time they'd get better at the whole Dom/sub dynamic of their relationship.

Then Tim left.

Now, eighteen months later, Craig's life was a wasteland, and he had tired of it. Tired of being tired. Tired of being angry and miserable and feeling like a total failure. He needed to get out of his head. He needed to break the sick cycle of thinking that had him awake most nights.

Craig stepped out of the cab a few blocks from the club and walked the rest of the way. He kept his head down and stuffed his hands in his pockets and returned to the club he'd visited a few days ago to set up a membership.

Most places used the same basic set up, go in one door, sign in while they reminded you of the basic rules, gave you a color-coded club standard BDSM wrist band indicating Dom or a sub, available or unavailable. Then you got to enter the world of kink unfettered.

Craig hated places like these, but they were better than meeting someone on a random app. He didn't like the idea of meeting a *complete* stranger who liked to tie people up. At least the club provided a controlled environment with people employed to keep their patrons safe.

It was little comfort.

Craig ordered a juice from the bar and looked around. He'd already been here once, for a few minutes, but during the day when the place was empty. Now it crawled with leather covered studs of all varieties. Craig raked his eyes over the crowd and took a deep breath. In a minute he'd get up the courage to throw himself into the fray. He drank his juice first, sipped it slowly until he emptied the glass. When he'd returned the glass, he took a deep breath. In another minute he'd slip into his sub mindset and maybe then a hot Dom would approach him and make him soar and forget about Tim.

Tim, whose eyes met his.

Tim, who he hadn't seen in eighteen months stood ten feet from him. He looked at Craig with wide eyes and a slack jaw. Someone next to Tim put a hand on his shoulder and leaned in. That's when Craig noticed the thick, black collar around Tim's neck.

Tim had a Dom.

Tim was a sub.

Before Craig could wrap his mind around Tim being a sub, or a switch, or there, ten feet from him, Tim moved closer. Craig stood stock still like a cornered rabbit, too afraid to move.

The juice in Craig's stomach churned. He didn't understand anything anymore. He'd avoided all the clubs Tim used to drag him to for this exact reason. It wasn't fair. Tim left him and now, the one time he'd gathered the courage to enter a club, Tim not only turned up, but as a fucking sub. A collared sub with a mammoth-sized Dom.

Only a few feet from him, Tim stopped. His *master's* hand lay on his shoulder and Craig's fist tightened. The fact that Tim had a master enraged him as much as it confused him.

"Craig. It's good to see you. How are you?" Tim smiled, but Craig knew him well enough to know that it was fake, as fake as the rest of him. Betrayal fuelled Craig's anger. He wanted to be anywhere but here.

"Go fuck yourself." Craig turned to leave, but a hand on his shoulder stopped him.

"You're a nasty little sub, aren't you? That's my boy you swore at and I expect you to apologize."

Craig spun around and knocked the Dom's hand off his shoulder. "Don't touch me. I'll talk to him however I want. I may be a sub, but I'm not your sub."

Tim didn't say anything. He stood there and let his master grab at Craig and bark at him to apologize and he stood there and watched with complete disinterest. As if Craig never mattered to him at all.

Craig glared at Tim as angry tears sprang to his eyes. He didn't care if Tim saw him cry, it wouldn't be the first time. "You're a piece of cowardly shit."

"I told you not to talk to my boy like that."

Craig flinched at the Dom's voice. Powerful and commanding, the tone was also edged with a bit of anger. Craig took a step back. "Screw you." He knew he shouldn't get so mouthy with a Dom, but his heart hammered as his vision blurred. At the same time, he couldn't catch his breath. Worse, his brain didn't appear to be in control of his mouth anymore and he heard himself yell. "Screw you and screw him too." Craig turned to leave, but the Dom caught his arm.

Before he could wonder what would happen next, another man came over and pulled the Dom's hand off Craig's arm.

"What's the trouble over here?" He had to be a Dom. Not as tall or as wide as Tim's giant of a man, he oozed a certain presence and had to be important because the angry Dom suddenly curbed his attitude.

"This little sub here seems to have a problem with my boy. They exchanged words and I want him to apologize."

"Fuck you, you shit." Craig's voice cracked. "And fuck him too." Craig panted, and fresh tears streamed down his cheeks. The other Dom appeared to be trying to spin it to make him look like the bad guy, and he might be, but all he wanted to do was leave. The guy should've let him go.

A hand touched his shoulder. "Kneel down, boy."

Craig dropped to his knees without giving it a thought. He didn't dare disobey that voice. That deep, smooth baritone that didn't bark at him to obey as the first Dom had done, but commanded obedience nonetheless.

The Dom put a hand on Craig's head and smoothed his fingers through his short brown hair. "Breathe, boy. Just breathe."

Craig no longer obeyed on instinct alone. He found himself wanting to please the man who came to his rescue.

"What's going on here?"

Craig heard the Dom start to answer, but he got cut off by the second Dom. "I want to hear it from your boy. What did you say to him to upset him?"

"Nothing, Sir." Tim almost stammered.

"Nothing?" Craig heard the total disbelief in the Dom's voice. "Didn't look like nothing." The Dom stroked his fingers through Craig's hair and Craig took another deep breath, one that somehow helped release the pressure on his lungs. "One minute the boy is at the bar, then you come sauntering over and he goes ten shades whiter and I want to know why."

"I was only saying hello." Tim mumbled, and Craig stiffened. He wanted to get to his feet and punch him in the face. Or grab him and demand answers. Or run away. Then the gentle fingers continued stroking his scalp; he understood the silent command and forced himself to relax.

"I think it was more than that." A tense silence followed, and part of Craig wanted to lift his head so he could see what was going on, but he kept his head bowed and his eyes lowered. He knew that if he looked at Tim, he'd lose it all over again. "I'm going to insist that you leave this sub alone from now on."

"But…"

"Do not argue with me, boy." When the second Dom spoke to Tim in that tone, Craig's blood heated with arousal. "The boy is obviously distressed and whatever the reason, you're the cause. Do not approach him again. Get your boy out of here, Paul, he's pissing me off and so are you. I better not hear so much as a whisper that you've talked to, looked at or approached this boy in any manner. Do you get me?"

Silence.

"Come on, boy. Time to play."

Craig lifted his gaze enough to watch two sets of feet turn and leave. Then he buried his face in his hands.

The hand that had been playing with his hair smoothed down his back. "You okay, boy?"

Craig couldn't respond. His throat squeezed shut with despair. He shook his head instead.

"It's okay. I'll take care of you." Craig didn't protest as the Dom pulled Craig to his feet. Shame burned through him and he bowed his head to hide his tear stained face. He couldn't believe that he lost it in front of everyone. Craig melted into the warmth offered by the Dom's arm when it slid around his waist. He found himself being led into the back through an area that was marked EMPLOYEES ONLY. The noise in the club faded a bit, then all but disappeared when the Dom kicked a door shut behind them.

The Dom took a seat on an oversized sofa and pulled Craig down next to him. He slipped his fingers through Craig's hair and cradled him against his chest. Despite his efforts to compose himself, Craig broke down. He clutched the Dom and let the tears come. He whispered soothing words to Craig and when his sobs softened, and his breathing evened out, he didn't disobey the sweet Dom when he gave him one more command.

"Sleep, boy. I've got you."

2
Alan

ALAN CLOCKED THE BOY the minute he'd set foot in the club. He looked not only shy and unsure, but half terrified, and that was before Paul and Tim approached him. Then the kid went white as a sheet. Alan didn't know exactly what happened, but the minute the boy knocked Paul's hand off his shoulder, he knew he'd have to step in.

By the time he'd dislodged himself from another over-eager sub looking to get him back into the scene, and made his way over to the trio, the kid was already falling to pieces. He had to admire him though; he thought as he raked his fingers through the boy's short hair. He'd been totally unwilling to take shit from Paul. He could still hear the venom in the words he'd hurled at the pair. Whatever had gone on between them, it started long before tonight.

Alan leaned back and kept the boy cradled against his chest. Whoever he was, this boy was exhausted, probably lost and wounded, probably by Paul's sub. There had to be a history there, but for the life of him he couldn't figure out what. Paul and Tim first appeared separately about two years ago. They did a few scenes together, then they entered into a trial contract. The Dom collared Tim eighteen months ago. Where the kid came into the picture, he had no idea.

Wherever he fit in, and whoever he was, Alan intended to find out. A sweet looking boy, with long eyelashes, pale skin, and brown hair. The sub had a tight body, not too tall, great ass. Alan wanted to know his name. He wanted to make him smile, and beg, and let go of the hurt that weighed him down.

Alan felt the boy stir in his arms. He looked down at the boy who looked up at him with sleepy, red-rimmed eyes. They were as brown as his hair and filled with infinite and equal amounts of anger and sadness.

"How are you feeling, boy?"

The boy made no move to dislodge himself from Alan's arms, so he carded his fingers through the boy's hair again.

"I'm a little better, Sir."

God, that word was music on that kid's lips. Compared to Alan he was a kid. He couldn't be more than twenty-five. Alan had reached thirty-five and was careening head first, full speed ahead toward forty.

"What's your name, boy?"

"Craig, Sir."

Alan took a deep breath. He had to play this just right. "My name is Alan. Did you drive here, Craig?"

"No, Sir. I took a cab."

"Are you hungry?"

The boy chewed on his lower lip for a minute. "A little, Sir."

"Okay, then here's what we're going to do. I'm going to send someone for your coat and we're going to slip out the back and head down the street to my friend's restaurant. When we get there, we'll eat, and when you're ready, you're going to tell me what happened out there." Alan felt Craig stiffen. "I'm sorry, but I really must insist. If there's a problem in my club, or with one of my members, I need to know. It's my responsibility to keep everyone safe. Do you understand?"

Alan forced himself to remain calm despite his heart hammering against his ribs and his stomach doing loop-the-loops. He feared that any second the spell this too-beautiful-to-be-true boy was under would break and Craig would scramble out of his arms.

Then the kid nodded and if Alan weren't desperately straining to hear any stray syllable that slipped out of Craig's lips, he might have missed the very quiet, *Yes, Sir.*

"Good boy." Alan didn't miss the spark of satisfaction in Craig's eyes at those words. He dragged his thumb over Craig's cheek. His cock took an interest a long time ago, but it was his whole body that twitched when Craig leaned into his touch. He wet his lips. "I'm going to have to move you for a minute, boy. I'm going to call for your jacket and then we'll go, okay?"

"Yes, Sir."

Craig didn't move. He seemed content in Alan's arms as he waited. With reluctance, Alan let go of Craig. But he smoothed a hand through the boy's hair before standing. He wondered why he couldn't seem to stop touching him. Sure, he was beautiful, but Alan had been around a long time. He'd seen plenty of beautiful subs before. Subs far nicer looking than Craig who looked a bit too pale and far too tired for his liking.

Alan shot a quick text to his doorman and requested him to find Craig's jacket and bring it to the back.

The jacket arrived a moment later and Craig slid into it. Unlike a lot of subs, Craig had shown up fully dressed. That alone brought him to Alan's attention. In a sea of leather and skin, a beautiful young man in a shiny black shirt stood out. And it added to the mystery. Not only was Alan desperate to know who Craig was and how he knew Tim and Paul, but he wanted to find out what lay under the shirt. Alan wanted to understand what caused the hurt he saw in his eyes and the exhaustion that seeped out of him.

"This way, boy." Alan knew he should stop calling him that, but he'd been so angry when Paul put his hands on the boy that his inner Dom had kicked into high gear and he could barely keep the voice in his head at bay that wanted to chant *mine mine mine mine mine.*

"No one will see us, right, Sir?"

Alan put his hand on Craig's shoulder. "That's right. If they are still around, they won't be back here." Alan smiled when Craig relaxed a little and let himself be led out of the building and around the corner until they were back onto the still busy street.

He took Craig to The Dragon's Den and with a nod to the hostess, they got seated immediately. Alan's friend kept a table reserved for him at all times. He and Steve went all the way back to high school, and it worked out nicely now. Alan always had a reservation at one of the hottest restaurants in the city, and Steve didn't have to pay for his membership at Alan's club.

The man himself appeared a moment later. He flicked his gaze to Craig, who had stripped out of his jacket, and Alan shook his head. They had a silent conversation the way only the best of friends can.

He yours?

No, but don't touch.

Got it.

"Long time no see." Steve beamed. He ignored Craig as per Alan's silent warning and pulled his friend into a hug. "You're lucky you got dibs, he's hot." He whispered in Alan's ear.

"I'll explain later," Alan whispered back. He pulled out of the hug and sank into the chair opposite Craig. "Can we get two ice waters and a couple of bacon double cheeseburgers." The restaurant didn't even serve burgers, but Steve insisted they made them special for Alan.

"Coming right up." Steve turned and vanished. He was good at gauging Alan's moods and Steve guessed that Alan wanted to be alone with Craig.

"So, Craig, what do you do for a living?"

"I'm a concierge at a hotel down town, Sir."

"We're not at the club anymore, Craig. You can call me Alan."

Craig nodded, and Alan watched as he sat a bit taller and reached for his water after it arrived. Some of the residual tension began to leave, but not the melancholy in his eyes which held firm. Alan found himself desperate to discover what Craig looked like when he smiled.

"How long have you been at the hotel?"

"Ten years."

Alan furrowed his brow. "Ten years? How old are you?"

The corner of Craig's lip turned up, it wasn't even a smirk, but it was the closest thing Alan had seen to a smile, to any sort of amusement or happy emotion since he first laid eyes on him. "I'm twenty-three, but my uncle owns the hotel and I started young."

"Why?"

Craig shrugged. "It was something to do, to be honest. My Mom died and my uncle took me in. I needed something to keep me busy during the summer because if I stopped to think too much . . ." Craig took a long drink of his water. "I started in the laundry room and worked my way up from there. So, Alan, what do you do at the club? I'm assuming you work there."

Alan forced a smile. "It's mine."

Craig stopped moving. He blinked and paled a little, not that Alan would've thought that possible. "Yours?"

"Mine." Like you, Alan wanted to add, but didn't. He wanted this boy. Wanted him with every part of his body, every bit of his soul felt attracted to Craig. Alan took a deep breath and opted for full disclosure. If Craig was going to open up to him, Alan would have to take that first step. "I purchased it with my partner twelve years ago. When we split up, I bought him out and now I run it alone." Alone. Alan hated that word. He lived alone. Ran the club alone. Ate alone. Sure, he had friends and he used to do the odd scene with a sub now and then, but a handful of scattered scenes would never fulfil Alan. In fact, his last scene had ended early. He'd had a gorgeous little sub tied to a cross, but when it came time to pick up the flogger, Alan couldn't. He'd felt completely unaffected by the sub and it stirred an emptiness inside him he still hadn't been able to shake. That was months ago, and Alan had yet to try another scene.

The cheeseburgers arrived, and the conversation halted as Craig eyed his burger. "This looks amazing."

Alan watched as Craig lifted the burger to his mouth and took a bite. Then Craig fucking moaned and Alan's already interested cock twitched. He shifted and did his best to ignore his discomfort.

They ate their burgers in silence, except for the occasional moan from Craig. If Alan didn't know any better, he'd have sworn the kid was doing it on purpose. The idea that he might be pleased Alan to no end.

Alan waited until they were both picking at their fries to bring up the subject of Paul and Tim.

"So, Craig, do you care to explain what happened back there in the club?" Alan's heart sank as he watched Craig shrink into himself. His shoulders rolled forward, and his gaze dropped to the floor. He started to reach for a fry, but then pulled a trembling hand back and tucked it down into his lap and out of sight.

"Not really."

"Would it help if we were somewhere more private, boy?" Alan tacked the endearment onto the end of his question so Craig would know this conversation wasn't an option. The only choice Craig had was where he felt comfortable having it.

"Yes, Sir."

"I'd suggest the club, but there tend to be interruptions. Would it be okay with you if we went back to my place?"

Craig's eyes lifted and met Alan's and for a flash of a second they didn't look quite as melancholy.

"Yes, Sir."

3

Craig

When Craig set foot in the club earlier he never imagined running into Tim or anything that happened afterward. But if his not-so-awesome run-in with his ex got him to where he stood, inside Alan's amazing house, he almost couldn't complain.

His heart hadn't stopped jack-hammering since Alan had leaned forward a little in his seat at the restaurant. When Craig heard the words, *my place* come out of the man's mouth, he nearly whimpered. Alan was gorgeous. A few inches taller than Craig's five foot eleven, compared to Craig's slender form, Alan was broad. But what Craig liked the best were Alan's blue eyes. He liked the crows feet that appeared at the corners when Alan smiled. When he'd been curled up with him at the club, he wanted to reach up and run his fingers through Alan's dark hair to see if it was as soft as it looked.

Alan's fingers skimmed over Craig's shoulders as he gently

stripped him out of his jacket. Craig turned his head and glanced at Alan over his shoulder.

"Let's skip the grand tour for now and get right to it."

Craig's breath hitched, and Alan grinned at him.

"Coffee? Tea? Soda? I'm afraid I don't drink, and I don't often have company, so I don't have any booze on hand."

"Tea would be fine, thank you, Sir." Craig turned his head so Alan couldn't see his face anymore. Alan seemed to like it when Craig called him Sir, but then again, what Dom didn't like it? When Alan told Craig to use his name, he thought it might be strange, but it rolled off his tongue and it made his insides shiver in a funny delicious sort of way. Craig had the feeling that only *certain* people in Alan's life got to use his name and he felt more than a little special at the thought that he might be one of those *certain* people. Even if it was only for one night.

Craig took a seat on one of the tall stools at the counter and looked around at Alan's home, what he could see of it from his location. It was a stunning home. Tall ceilings, nicely decorated, but not too nicely. It wasn't a scary, cold, catalogue type place that made Craig afraid to touch anything. It was warm and inviting and rather homey, he thought.

He watched Alan as he prepared a tray. First with a couple cups, then with a creamer and a sugar bowl. Finally, a teapot. And when the water was heated, Alan dropped a few bags into the pot and filled it with the hot water.

"Follow me, we'll have a seat in the den."

He followed behind Alan and watched him walk. He loved the way he moved, so graceful and methodical. Craig found himself admiring the way Alan's ass flexed in his black slacks. His face flushed when Alan bent over and set the tray on a coffee table. The way Alan's muscles contracted when he bent reminded him of how good it felt to be in his arms.

Alan turned his head and Craig felt his blush deepen. Part of him hoped Alan would pull him into his lap. He liked the way Alan's arms felt when they wrapped around him, but being in the same room as Alan was a high in and of itself. He felt safe around him.

A fantasy of what it could be like, to have everything he ever wanted, unfolded in a split second. He imagined Alan taking care of him the way he'd always wanted. Well, not always, but definitely since he stumbled across that blog. Something inside him clicked into place when he read the posts written by *HisDaddysGoodBoy889*. Alan was calm, but strong, and he made him feel safe. He could be the perfect Daddy.

Craig snapped out of his daydream when Alan motioned to the large recliner opposite to the one he sat on. "Please, sit."

Craig all but scurried over to the chair and plopped into it. He clasped his hands in his lap to still them. He was fidgety by nature and it only became worse when he got nervous, or excited, or scared, or… okay, so maybe he was always a bit fidgety.

Alan poured two cups of tea and Craig added a single spoon of sugar to his. He didn't like things that were too sweet. Then he remembered that Alan didn't bring him here for idle chit chat about his job or the weather. He wanted to know what went on in the club—his club. Craig almost snorted, but he did shake his head.

"You look almost amused about something. Care to share, boy?" Alan's tone was gentle and while Craig knew that he was a Dom and had already witnessed a scrap of his commanding Dom persona, he didn't doubt that Alan's gentle nature went all the way to his core.

"I thought that it was a bit… funny, ironic I guess… I don't *like* clubs."

"And yet you were in one tonight."

Craig shrugged. "It's safer to meet someone who could…" he shrugged and brought his tea to his lips to cut off the rest of his sentence.

"Who could what?"

Craig inhaled and fought the urge to close his eyes. The hard edge was back to Alan's voice as he switched into full on Dom mode. And be damned if Craig didn't want to kneel at his feet and beg for anything the Dom was willing to give him. He took a breath and stared down into his tea as he answered. "Who could take care of me, Sir."

Craig waited and for a moment he thought for sure Alan would ask him *exactly* what it was he was looking for. But Alan took a drink of his tea and leaned back in his chair.

"How do you know Paul and Tim?"

Craig flinched and forced himself to take a deep breath. "Tim was my Dom, Sir."

Alan's eyebrows rose up in shock, then crashed down in confusion. "Your Dom? He must be a switch then. What happened with you two?"

"Truthfully. I don't exactly know, Sir." Craig took a sip of his tea, grateful he had it to cling to, to keep his hands busy.

Taking a drink gave him time to pause and collect his thoughts while trying to tamp down the misery that still wanted to bubble out of him. "I came home a year and a half ago and he was gone. All his things, it was as if he was never even there to begin with. He quit his job and changed his number. He just . . . vanished."

Craig took a sip of his tea and willed himself not to fall apart again. Sobbing in Alan's arms more than once on their first meeting was a few miles beyond the border of totally pathetic. "He left a note, but it didn't explain much. Not really. I knew we were having problems, but I thought we'd have time to work on them." He took a deep breath, and it shuddered out of him. "That's how I know Tim, Sir. I have no idea who Paul is."

"Paul is his Dom."

Craig raised his gaze and met Alan's. "I think he hates me, Sir."

"You're likely right, but don't take it personally. Paul doesn't like anyone who has already had what he owns. Tell me, boy," Alan set his mug down then leaned back again. "Do you miss him?"

"Yes and no, Sir."

Alan's mouth twitched. "Well, thanks for clearing that up."

Craig liked this new side of Alan. The gentle teasing helped to ease some of his distress. "Sometimes I miss him, usually when I forget that I shouldn't miss someone who thought so little of me that they abandoned me with no warning and left only a shitty note to explain. Then I remember to be angry at him and I don't miss him as much when I'm angry at him."

"Why did you come to my club tonight?"

"Well, I certainly wasn't looking for Tim, Sir." Craig scoffed. "The one club I pick because we never went there and there wouldn't be memories, and he's right fucking there." Craig flinched. "Sorry, Sir. I didn't mean to swear."

Alan waved it off. "It's okay, boy. I'd swear, too. But you still haven't answered the question. Why did you come to the club?"

Craig shut his eyes. He found it helped him say the things he had trouble saying if he could close his eyes and pretend that maybe the words weren't coming out of his mouth. And if your eyes were closed, you never had to worry about seeing their reaction. "I've been alone for a long time, too long. I'm ready to move on. I wanted . . . I hoped to find someone to look after me, at least for a little while."

"So you went to my club, hoping to meet a Dom who would take one look at your tight little body and snatch you up. You were looking for someone to make you feel good and forget all about what's-his-name?"

It took Craig half a minute to get the words to whisper past his lips. "Yes, Sir."

"What if I told you that not only could I make you feel good, but that I could make you fly?"

Craig's head snapped up, and he caught the Dom's heated gaze. His palms instantly got damp, and he set the mug on the coffee table in case he started shaking. "Sir?"

"It would only be tonight, so I wouldn't bother with a contract. I don't have anything too heavy in mind, but you could tell me your safe word anyway, for the sake of protocol. I don't make a habit of sleeping with my subs, so you don't need to worry if I'm clean or not, we won't be going *that* far."

"Let me see if I understand this, Sir. You want to do a scene with me, but not anything too intense, so you're tossing out the need for a contract, because it's only for tonight. You're not going to fuck me and I'm assuming I'm not going to fuck you and you say you can make me feel good?"

Alan nodded.

For the first time in forever, Craig smiled. "Sounds perfect, Sir."

Alan rose to his feet and held his hand out to Craig. "Come with me."

"Yes, Sir."

Alan led him up the stairs and into a bedroom. He doubted that it was Alan's room, it was furnished with a queen-sized bed and a dresser and had very few decorations and absolutely no personal touches.

"I'll be right back. While I'm gone, I want you to undress. You can fold your clothes and stack them on the dresser. Lay face down on the bed when you're done."

"Yes, Sir."

The minute Alan was gone Craig whipped his shirt off. He folded it and placed it neatly on the dresser. He paused for a moment and questioned if he should be doing this or not, but Craig immediately brushed the thought aside. They were doing something light, something so light that they hadn't even really discussed Craig's limits. It sounded weird, but Alan owned a club, he doubted he could've ended up with a safer Dom . . . or at least with a Dom that made him feel as safe as Alan did.

By the time Alan returned, Craig lay sprawled out on the bed, face down, as instructed. He heard Alan put some things down on the dresser, but he'd have to move to see exactly what, and he didn't want to move. He wanted to please Alan.

Alan sat on the edge of the bed and Craig *did* whimper this time when Alan swept his fingers through his hair.

"Here's what's going to happen, boy. I'm going to blindfold you and I'm going to put earplugs in your ears. I'm going to take away those two senses and I want you to lie there and feel. You can make noise if you must, but you can't talk unless you ask me to stop. If you need me to stop, say so and I will. Is that okay?"

"Yes, Sir."

Alan's hand swept down Craig's spine and he did his best to lay still, but he arched up into Alan's touch, anyway. It had been so long since another man had touched him that he suddenly found himself knowing exactly what he'd been missing, and he felt starved for more.

"Lift your head a little, that's a good boy."

Craig lifted his head enough for Alan to get the blindfold in place. "Is that too tight?"

"No, Sir."

"I'm going to put the plugs in your ears now. They won't hurt, they're soft and foamy. Okay, boy?"

"Yes, Sir."

"I promise, while you're blindfolded and without your hearing that I will not leave this room."

"Thank you, Sir." Craig exhaled and found himself relieved that Alan promised not to leave him. It wasn't like he was bound and unable to move, but he was under Alan's control and he liked the reassurance that Alan wouldn't leave him, even for a second.

A moment later Craig was floating in a sea of nothing. His eyes were shut, but even if he opened them he'd see nothing but an inky darkness. His hearing was completely gone, but he knew Alan was still there, because he'd promised not to leave, and Craig trusted him in a way that a person probably shouldn't trust an almost stranger.

The first thing he felt was the bed dip as Alan climbed on. Then he straddled him. Craig's thighs were sandwiched between Alan's. Two warm and slick hands stroked over his shoulders and Craig thought he might die of shock. Alan was giving him a massage. He took a deep breath and exhaled a little more of his tension and he could've sworn that he felt Alan laugh.

Craig all but melted into the mattress as Alan's powerful hands massaged his shoulders, then followed the length of his spine. He worked his way down Craig's back. His powerful hands, slick with massage oil, eased all the tension out of Craig. He wasn't even thinking anymore. His brain was blissfully blank. The only thoughts taking up residence there were of the hands that worked agonizingly closer to his ass.

Then Alan shuffled down the bed and those gorgeous hands *did* touch his ass and then that became the only thought in Craig's head. The other man's powerful hands dug into the muscles and Craig moaned. He didn't care if he sounded like a shameless slut, it had been ages since anyone touched him at all and now those amazing hands touched Craig everywhere.

His cock had also been paying attention to Alan's hands and fully erect, squashed into the mattress. Craig wanted to buck his hips and give into the delicious friction, but he didn't have permission. He didn't want to risk doing anything to disappoint Alan and end this glorious massage.

Alan's hands left Craig's ass and worked their way down his legs and Craig doubted that he could buck his hips even if he tried. He felt boneless and weightless, as if he was made of liquid all over—well, maybe not all over. One part of him was still very stiff and solid. Then Alan rolled him over, straddled his hips and started massaging his chest in wide, slow, circles.

Oh shit. Craig thought as Alan's clothed cock almost brushed against his. He was sad that Alan didn't grind himself into Craig, because it would've surely felt delicious, but he was also glad because he was so hard and desperate and aching that one stray touch would probably send him flying and he didn't want to come like a teenager with a hair trigger.

Alan's hands worked lower and glided up and down his torso now. Half delirious from pleasure and half crazy with need, Craig begged. He begged and pleaded for Alan to touch him, to make him come. He needed it, needed Alan. Then a warm, slick hand wrapped around his cock and Craig's world went white with ecstasy.

4
Alan

ALAN HAD NEVER SEEN a sight more beautiful than Craig. When he rolled the boy over and started massaging his chest he was completely pliant under his touch. Alan's cock was rock solid almost to the point of being painful. Being trapped in his trousers didn't make things any easier. From the moment he first touched Craig and the boy whimpered and then relaxed, Alan wanted him. He wanted him relaxed, and happy, and begging. Then Alan rolled him over and Craig's breathing became shallow and needy. His beautiful cock was rock solid, and it was all he could do to ignore it. This wasn't supposed to be about that. This was supposed to be a simple massage, something to relax Craig and help him float for a while and hopefully forget about that bastard Tim.

Then Craig whimpered again.

"Please, Sir. Please. Please." Craig's voice was thick with need and his eyebrows started to draw together. The poor boy was aching for release. Alan ran his hands down Craig's torso. He loved the way Craig's muscles seemed to chase his touch.

"Please, Sir. Please. I need . . . I need . . ."

Alan couldn't resist. Craig was too beautiful laying there, shiny and slick with oil. His face a perfect combination of bliss and need, his body taut, muscles twitching.

"Please, Sir. Touch me, please. Please, Sir."

Alan wrapped his hand around Craig's cock and even then Craig made no move to chase more friction. The boy was totally and completely immersed in his submission and fuck, he was so perfect Alan could've cried. He stroked his oil slick hand up Craig's cock. He loved the way Craig's lips parted as he panted and moaned.

Alan tightened his grip on Craig's cock and stroked upward. He added a bit of a twist and finally, Craig fell apart, bit by bit. He bit back a moan, his hips thrust up slightly, then he slammed them back down and forced himself not to move. Alan stroked him again, and Craig's head tilted back, his back arched, his hips bucked and spurts of cum splattered his beautiful stomach.

Alan reached for the box of tissues he'd left on the dresser and dutifully mopped the cum off Craig's stomach and cock. Normally he would've preferred to use his tongue, but Alan didn't want to go too far. He'd only met Craig recently and he didn't want to do anything to scare the boy or chase him away, and judging from the way his breathing had evened out, Craig was asleep.

Alan carefully got up off the bed and turned the light off. When he climbed back onto the bed he pulled Craig into his arms and carefully removed the ear plugs and the blindfold. God, it felt good to have someone in his arms. It had been so long since Alan got to take care of someone he almost forgot how fantastic it felt. It amazed him that Craig trusted him as much as he did, but he'd be a liar if he said he was anything but thrilled.

Craig seemed to be coming back to earth in increments. Then Craig turned a little in his arms until he was tucked in against Alan. He wrapped an arm around Alan's middle and snuggled into him even more.

"Thank you, Sir." He mumbled sleepily.

"I guess that means you enjoyed yourself, boy?"

Alan looked down at Craig, who had opened his eyes and Alan found himself wishing he would've left the light on so he could see him better. He wanted to look into his eyes and see if he'd managed to chase away even a fraction of the pain he'd seen there earlier. No one so young, so beautiful, and so sweet should walk around with so much anger and devastation in their eyes.

"Yes, Sir." Craig closed his eyes and snuggled into Alan. "Thank you, Sir."

Alan smoothed his hand through Craig's hair and he nearly came in his pants when Craig let out a content sigh. God, this boy was beyond perfect. Sweet and submissive and so fucking responsive. Alan found himself irate that Tim had treated this precious boy so horribly. Then he hated himself for allowing even a little gratitude to poke its way in. If it weren't for Tim, Craig wouldn't be here, cradled sleepily against Alan's chest.

"Sir?"

"What is it, boy?"

Craig said something, but he was clearly embarrassed or unsure about it, because even though Alan had been listening, he wasn't able to make out what he said. He ran his fingers down Craig's cheek and traced the edge of his jaw. Then he tilted Craig's face up and looked down at him.

"You'll have to speak up a little, boy."

Craig kept his eyes shut, but he managed to speak a little louder this time. "Can I . . . can I stay here tonight, Sir? I'm not ready to go home yet. Please, Sir."

Craig's voice cracked on the word please and Alan's heart damn near split in half and broke for the sweet little sub. In the next moment though, Alan grinned from ear to ear. He leaned down to press a kiss to the boy's forehead. "Of course, you can stay. I'll clean you up and . . . if you'd like, you can sleep with me."

That made Craig open his eyes. "With you, Sir?"

"Yes, my sweet boy. I want you next to me tonight, but first I want to hold you a little longer. Is that okay?"

Craig smiled and tucked himself down once again so his head rested on Alan's chest. "Yes, Sir. It's more than okay."

Alan held Craig for a while longer. He carded his fingers through Craig's hair. He stroked his arm and his back and any part of the boy he could comfortably reach. He catalogued all of Craig's little reactions. His delicate whimpers when Alan touched a sensitive spot. The tiny flinches when he happened upon a particularly ticklish patch of skin.

Alan curbed his reluctance and decided it was time to get them into the bath.

"Come on. Bath time, boy." Alan knew he should switch back to calling him Craig. Alan wasn't his Dom, Craig wasn't his sub, but be damned if he didn't like the way Craig responded to it.

"Yes, Sir."

Alan shifted Craig out of his arms and told himself that he didn't instantly miss the feeling of the smaller man pressed against him. He climbed off the bed and produced a robe for Craig. "Up, boy. Let's get you to the tub."

Craig rose to his feet and allowed Alan to help him into the robe. Alan had to rein in his urge to grab Craig, wrap his arms around him and kiss him senseless. He needed to know if his lips were as soft as they looked. He wondered what kind of sounds the boy would make when Alan slid his tongue into his mouth. He wanted to know if he'd lean into the kiss, or turn into beautiful submissive putty in Alan's hands.

Craig leaned dutifully against the counter and watched Alan as he poured the bath. When Alan reached for the top button of his shirt Craig pushed off the counter.

"May I, Sir?"

Alan forced himself not to grin like an idiot. "You may."

Craig came forward, still draped in Alan's robe. It was much too big for him, but Alan liked how he looked in it. The sleeves draped down to his finger tips and the robe went halfway down his calves. His boy looked so small and sweet and positively edible in it.

Alan twitched. *His boy.* He wanted to pretend that he didn't know the exact moment he'd begun to think of the sweet sub as his, but he did. That first command. *Kneel down, boy.* Craig sank to his knees and Alan had brushed his fingers through the boy's hair and when Alan felt him sag with relief, he'd latched onto the boy and he found himself wanting to keep him. The connection he felt was instant and electric.

Alan waited patiently while his boy undid each of his buttons, then his cuffs and slid the shirt off his shoulders. He folded it neatly before returning to start on Alan's pants. His boy was sweet, methodical, and not properly trained, Alan noted. Alan found the lack of experience endearing. It was the little things he did, like the way he'd sneak too many glances at Alan's face, rather than always keeping his eyes downcast until ordered otherwise. He liked that he was forward enough to ask for things, most subs Alan had come across knew his reputation as a Dom and would never be so bold as to ask if they were allowed to undress him. But his boy was sweet, and he liked how comfortable he was with him.

It had surprised Alan a little to learn that he didn't like the club scene. And it surprised Alan even further when he felt a little sigh of relief. It was something he'd have to think about later when his boy wasn't gently stripping him out of his pants.

When he was naked, and his clothes were neatly folded and stacked on the counter, Alan stripped his boy out of the robe and helped him into the tub. He climbed in behind him and pulled Craig against his chest. He cradled the boy in his arms and shut his eyes. He could get used to this, he thought, to having Craig around, to having him in his arms and in his bath and in his bed.

Alan squeezed some body wash into his hands and rubbed it into Craig's smooth skin. If he were cleansing himself he'd have used a cloth, but he wanted to feel the smooth exposed skin under his hands. Satisfied that he'd washed all the oil off, he placed an impulsive kiss on the top of Craig's shoulder.

"Okay, out we get. It's time for bed, boy."

"Yes, Sir."

Craig climbed out of the tub, and like a good little sub, he handed Alan two towels. Alan took one and wrapped it around his waist. He grabbed the other and gently dabbed it all over Craig's body. With the boy dry, Alan wrapped the towel around Craig's waist before drying himself off.

"I'll give you something to sleep in. I have some lounge wear, it'll be a little large on you." Alan was desperate to feel the boy's skin against his. He took him by the hand and led him into his room where he grabbed a pair of lounge pants out of the top drawer and handed them to Craig.

"I don't think I could contain myself with that sweet little naked ass pressed up against me all night. Into the pants you get, boy." Alan grinned at the flush of pink that swept up Craig's chest, cheeks and even tinted the tops of his ears.

"What if I didn't want you to be a gentleman, Sir?"

Oh, fuck. This little sub was going to kill him. Alan bit back a groan and cupped Craig's cheek in his hand. He didn't want the boy to feel bad over the rejection, because it was anything but that. It was the opposite. The boy was vulnerable tonight and he didn't want to take advantage. So far Alan felt confident that he'd stayed on the right side of this, but pinning the boy down and fucking him into the mattress would cross that line. He simply didn't want to fuck this up. "Tonight isn't about that, boy."

When Craig's eyes dropped down to look at the floor, Alan tugged him into his arms and kissed the top of his head. "You've been so good, and so sweet, but you've also had a really long, hard day, haven't you, boy?"

"Yes, Sir."

"Tonight, I'm going to hold you and we're going to go to sleep. In the morning I'm going to make you the best cup of coffee you've ever had and then we're going out for breakfast." Alan furrowed his brow. "Unless you have to work tomorrow. It is a weekday."

"I work weekends, Sir, when it's busier. I usually get Tuesday and Wednesday off."

"Good. Then put those on and crawl into bed."

Alan slid into bed and turned back the covers. He watched Craig slide into his pants. They both laughed when the pants slid down Craig's waist. They barely held onto his hips, one tiny tug would leave them in a puddle of fabric around his ankles. Craig hiked them up and held them with one hand while he crawled into bed.

Alan opened his arms and Craig went into them. He pressed his face into Alan's chest. Alan tucked them in and let himself indulge in touching Craig some more. He smoothed his hand up and down Craig's back and felt the boy relax. His breathing softened and evened out and for a moment Alan thought he was already sleeping.

"Thank you for everything, Sir." He whispered.

Alan's arms tightened around his boy and he lay awake for a long time, holding his boy in his arms and wondering exactly what he did to deserve this sweet boy. He hoped he could keep him for more than one night, because now Alan knew what it was that he'd been missing.

Him.

This.

Someone who needed him to do something other than flog him into subspace. Someone who needed comfort and protection and reassurance. Craig needed someone to talk to him, to be sweet to him and to comfort him and cuddle him. Alan needed someone who would let themselves be taken care of. Someone who wouldn't take Alan for granted, or be bratty to try to eke a punishment out of him. Alan wanted someone who wanted to submit, who relished it, no matter what that submission led to. Most of the subs he'd come across wanted a specific kind of domination. Flogging. Caning. Humiliation. If he was right, Craig wanted submission, he wanted to please, no matter what that meant at the time.

Alan didn't fall asleep for a long time. If he was only going to be given one night with this beautiful, perfect, sub, he was going to enjoy as much of it as he could.

5

Craig

CRAIG WOKE WITH THE sun on his face and with two strong arms twined around him. He snuggled closer to Alan and breathed deep. Thank god it hadn't been a dream. If Craig had woke in his own apartment, alone one more time, he might not have believed any of it happened at all. But here in Alan's house, in his bed and his arms he could breathe in the reality of it all.

And the reality was that Craig found more last night than he ever hoped for. When he entered that club, he expected to stumble on some sort of giant Dom who'd want to tie him up and flog him or maybe he'd want to put him in a cock cage and shove a butt plug up his ass and parade him around for a while before he fucked him senseless.

What he found was so much more than that. Kind and gentle, not only did Alan come to Craig's rescue, but he stayed with him afterward and made sure he was okay. He seemed to be genuinely interested in the events that led to the confrontation in the club, and not only because it was *his* club—something Craig would have to spend some time wrapping his head around. He got the impression Alan wanted to know what happened because he cared. Why he cared, Craig didn't know, but was glad he did.

He certainly never expected the Dom to climb on top of him and massage him into subspace. Then Craig remembered the grip around his cock, powerful and firm and not too much, but not too light. It had taken only a few strokes and Craig soared so high so fast that the only way to recover was to immediately fall asleep. And waking up in Alan's arms the first time had felt almost as good as—and maybe even better than—his orgasm.

Craig's stomach clenched. and he squeezed his eyes shut. Alan took care of him last night in a way that no one ever had before. Was this what it was like to belong to someone? Was this what it felt like to have a Daddy? Craig exhaled a deep breath and tried not to dwell on it. It was only a pipe dream.

"I can hear you thinking." Alan mumbled. His voice thick with sleep was sexy as fuck. Craig's cock, which was already awake, twitched with renewed interest. He gave his ass a little wiggle and laughed when Alan put his hand on his hip and forced him to stay still.

"Is today not about that either?" Craig quipped. He wanted to sound pouty and indignant, but he couldn't keep the joy and the bliss out of his voice. It was only then that he realized that he'd come awake with a smile on his face . . . and that he actually slept all night long. Nights were usually spent restlessly tossing and turning and grabbing a few hours before dawn. Last night he'd fallen asleep so easily and slept so soundly that he almost felt like a different person. Or maybe he felt like his old self, but it had been so long he almost forgot what the old Craig was really like.

"Do you always think so hard first thing in the morning?"

"How can you tell I was thinking?" Alan had dropped the endearment which made Craig happy. While he loved being called boy, he wanted to be more than that to Alan. He didn't want to be nothing more than some kid Alan plucked up off the floor of the club and decided to play with.

"When you think too much you get all rigid and unresponsive."

Craig took a deep breath and made himself relax in Alan's arms. He didn't want to do anything to ruin this beautiful feeling. This bright, floaty feeling was the stuff that dreams were made of. But, all good things must come to an end.

"I have to pee." He rolled over, so he could see Alan's face. "And I'm pretty sure that you promised me coffee last night."

Alan reached up and brushed his fingers over Craig's cheek. He loved how tactile Alan acted with him. He loved being touched and petted. The way Alan touched him made him feel like there was something about him that was worth appreciating. "I did promise you that, didn't I." Alan leaned in and pressed a kiss to Craig's forehead. "First thing's first." Alan kissed him one more time, then seeming a little reluctant, pried himself away from Craig. "I'll use the bathroom downstairs and get the coffee going. You can use the ensuite again. There's a new toothbrush in the bottom drawer."

Craig watched as Alan strode to the dresser and pulled out a pair of lounge pants. He almost wished he'd stay naked, but at least his ass looked fabulous in the clingy fabric.

By the time Craig finished in the bathroom and made his way downstairs to the kitchen, Alan had the coffee started.

"Wow, does that ever smell good." Craig held onto the waistband of the borrowed pants so they wouldn't fall down again, and took a seat on the same stool he'd sat at last night. A lot had happened in the twelve hours that Craig had known Alan. Shit. Only twelve hours? Craig chewed on his lip and mulled it over. Yeah, it was about eight when he'd gone to the club and he met Alan shortly after entering. It was now a little after nine in the morning.

"Something wrong?"

"No, not all. I was thinking that... I'm really comfortable with you, you know. We only just met, but... I'm having a really nice time. You've been good to me and I was thinking that it was nice to connect with someone again." Craig dropped his gaze down to the floor, not out of submission, but embarrassment. He hadn't meant to say all that. But when he started talking, Alan smiled and the man's whole face seemed to glow with joy that shone out from inside of him. Craig found himself somewhat embarrassed that he'd said so much.

"I'm really glad you came to the club last night." Alan poured them both a cup of coffee. "Do you take milk or sugar?"

"And ruin the best coffee ever? Not a chance." Craig took the offered cup and gave it an appreciative sniff before taking a sip. "Shit, that's good."

Alan winked at him. "Told you." Alan took a drink of

his own. "So, do we need to run by your house and grab you something to wear before we go to breakfast?"

Craig winced. "I guess we should. Or... I could cook us something and we could stay in."

"What did you have in mind?"

"Do you have the stuff for omelettes?"

"I should, but are you sure you wouldn't rather go somewhere to eat?"

Craig felt his face heat. Normally he hated his tendency to blush, but Alan seemed to approve of the pink hue on his skin. "I think I'd rather stay here and hang out, if that's okay."

Alan smiled warmly and reached for Craig. Craig leaned into his touch when he stroked his thumb over Craig's cheek. He fought the urge to close his eyes and sigh. "That sounds like a fantastic idea." Alan pulled away and smiled at Craig. "Let me make a call. I'm taking the day off and we're going to hang out until you get sick of me. How does that sound?"

"Amazing." Craig wanted to scoff. Like he'd ever get sick of Alan.

Alan made his call while Craig washed his hands. By the time Alan came back into the room, Craig had stacked all the necessary ingredients on the counter. "Where do you keep your frying pans?"

Alan pointed to a cupboard and Craig bent to retrieve a pan. When he stood up, the too-large lounge pants fell to the floor. Craig blushed and hiked them back up with one hand. "Not sure I can cook with one hand though. Might prove to be a bit dangerous."

Alan laughed and crossed the room. He opened a drawer

and Craig laughed when he saw that it was crammed full of random junk. "I'm so glad you have one of those."

Alan cast a glance over his shoulder. "One of what?"

"A junk drawer. Seriously. It makes me feel miles better about my life. You own a club and you have an amazing house and you're so freaking hot. Your junk drawer makes you seem a little more human."

Alan laughed and shut the drawer. "Come here."

Craig crossed the room and nearly fainted when Alan dropped to his knees. Craig reached out and grabbed the counter to steady himself.

Alan's face was only a few inches from his dick, which really, really, enjoyed the close proximity.

Alan looked up at him with his beautiful blue eyes and Craig barely resisted the urge to run his fingers through Alan's dark hair. He didn't look thirty-five. Maybe it was because the dark hair didn't have a hint of grey, or maybe it was his smooth, youthful expression. His tongue poked out and slid over his lower lip, then he spoke in a low, husky voice. "Stay still."

Fingertips gently brushed against Craig's exposed stomach and he resisted the urge to flinch away from the touch. He was super ticklish in some places and unfortunately for him, his stomach happened to be one of those places.

Then, Alan rose to his feet and carded his fingers through Craig's hair. "There. All done."

Craig looked down and saw that Alan had secured his pants with a safety pin. It wasn't ideal, but at least they would stop falling.

"Be careful, okay. Don't forget that's in there. I don't want to see you get hurt."

Alan's soft expression gave away the deeper truth of the sentiment, but Craig decided that conversations like that were best had after breakfast, and after you'd known the person longer than half a day.

"I promise to be careful." *Daddy.* He bit his lip so the word wouldn't slip past. But in that moment, with Alan so gently and carefully taking care of him without a second thought, Craig wished Alan could be that for him.

"Good."

They fell into an easy rhythm. Craig cracked the eggs and whisked them together while Alan chopped some of the vegetables. He let Craig to do the cooking while he gathered a couple of plates from the cupboard. Craig found himself awe struck at how easy it was to be with Alan. They didn't seem to have a problem being comfortable with each other whether they were talking or not talking. The silences were as stress-free as the conversation.

When they sat down to eat, Alan sat on the stool next to Craig at the counter. They talked a little while eating. Nothing earth shattering, they made general conversation. Every time Alan's arm brushed against Craig's, or every time their legs bumped against each other, an odd little thrill shot up Craig's spine.

"Tell me about your uncle. What's he like?" Alan pushed his empty plate off to the side and turned in his seat so he could lean against the counter and look at Craig.

Craig pushed the last few bits of his omelette around his

plate. "He's . . . my uncle." He frowned. "I, uh," Craig stopped to take a deep breath. "He wasn't so good with the whole, raising a kid thing. He was a bachelor his whole life and he never had any interest in having a kid. It was a bit of an adjustment for him. He didn't really know what to do with me, and I suppose I didn't really know what to do with myself either."

"So he put you to work in the hotel?"

"Yeah. He paid me well though, and he taught me to be smart with my money. When I first started, he'd bank seventy-five percent of my paycheck and the other twenty five percent was my spending money. He told me that because he has money, it doesn't mean that I have money, and that if I wanted to be loaded like him, that I'd have to make my own fortune."

"Sounds like a smart guy."

Craig found himself smiling at that comment. Most people didn't have a favorable reaction to that story. They felt that his uncle was mean and nasty and greedy, but Craig's uncle wasn't mean. He didn't teach Craig how to manage money to be a jerk, he did it so Craig would be able to take care of himself. "Thanks. He is."

Craig finished the last bite of his omelette. "I think you'd like him. He's busy a lot of the time, but he pencils me in for dinner at the hotel whenever he can. Maybe you could come some time." Craig hopped off the stool and quickly gathered the plates. He headed to the sink, kicking himself the whole way for being so forward and full of assumptions. He didn't know if Alan wanted this to continue beyond today. For all he knew, this was a one-time thing.

"I'd like that."

Craig grinned and rinsed the plates in the sink before stacking them nicely in the dishwasher. He tried not to read too much into Alan's comment. He was only being nice. Oh, but it would be so easy for Craig to believe otherwise. He hoped Alan felt a fraction of the electricity between them that he did.

But Alan hadn't even kissed him, and maybe it was because Alan didn't kiss anyone. Craig had met guys like that before, guys who were all about the hook-ups, but that didn't fit Alan. Alan didn't seem like he was shirking away from intimacy. He'd spent the whole night petting and cuddling and touching Craig. So it had to be him. Alan simply didn't want to kiss him.

Determined not to dwell on that sad fact, Craig gave Alan a bright smile. "So, what's next on the agenda? The grand tour? I bet the rest of the place is as amazing as what I've seen so far. I bet you have a killer dungeon, right? Big bad Dom with the huge in-home dungeon for all his naughty little subs."

Alan got a strange look on his face, but he said nothing. He held his hand out for Craig to take. "Come here. I'll show you."

Craig furrowed his brow and took Alan's hand. Alan twined their fingers together and led him back toward the master bedroom. He opened the door to the room next to it and dropped Craig's hand. "That's the playroom. Check it out."

Craig didn't know what exactly he'd expected, but it sure wasn't this. He walked into the room and looked around as he turned in a slow circle. His gaze sought out Alan's. "It's the guest bedroom I was in last night."

Alan nodded. "Yes, not what you were expecting was it?

It's a very unassuming room. Mike and I seldom played at home and when we did we played in here. He said he couldn't get in the right head space when we played in our bedroom."

Craig frowned and crossed the room. He slid his arms around Alan's waist and leaned into him. He knew Alan liked touching him and unless he was wrong, Alan seemed uneasy about this.

"When I was with Mike, we did most of our playing at the club. We used this room for playing at home which didn't happen often. Neither one of us saw a point in constructing a big in-home playroom if we owned a club. When my relationship with Mike deteriorated and came to an end, I hit a bit of a rough patch. I played with a few different subs, but I never brought them home from the club and I didn't fuck them. I couldn't because none of them were right and it took awhile, but I eventually realized they weren't what I wanted anymore." Alan took a deep breath and smoothed his hands down Craig's back. "Mike was my sub and my business partner. We were together for quite a while and when it ended it took me a long time to realize my needs had changed. I didn't need a hardcore sub to scene with anymore. I didn't need the leather and the whips and the benches and the props and the toys. I didn't need any of that. I have some stuff here, bondage stuff mainly, a few of my favorite floggers, that kind of thing. I know, it seems fucked up for a Dom who owns a kink club to only have a few basic toys at home."

Craig tightened his arms around Alan. "It doesn't seem strange at all. It's not what you need, so why have a bunch of stuff here that you have no interest in using." He guessed that must be the reason Tim found it so easy to get rid of him. He wasn't what Tim needed anymore.

Craig flinched. He hated how thoughts of Tim had infiltrated his quiet moment with Alan. He was tired of thinking about Tim and obsessing over him. Tim had clearly moved on. If Craig wasn't determined to do so yesterday, fantasies of him and Alan waking up bathed in sunshine together redoubled his determination today.

He buried his face against Alan's chest and squeezed his eyes shut. He really wished he had the guts to kiss Alan, but if Alan really didn't want to kiss him, he doubted that he could handle the rejection gracefully enough to not totally ruin everything.

Instead of entertaining further thoughts of kissing, Craig looked up at Alan. "What kind of movies do you like?" Alan grinned and Craig felt relief when the strange look left the other man's face. If he had to put a name on the facial expression, he'd call it, *reluctant nostalgia of the melancholic variety*, something he was all too familiar with.

They spent the rest of their day curled up together on Alan's big sectional couch. Alan had a love for old action flicks and seemed horrified to find out Craig had never watched the *Die Hard* movies.

Craig would've been a liar if he said he was happy to get dressed and go home. He hated the thought of going home to his empty apartment and laying awake. Even as he pulled his pants up over his hips, he knew he was in for a long night of staring at the ceiling.

Alan didn't seem very enthusiastic to get rid of him either.

Or maybe Craig was projecting his own disappointment onto Alan, but either way, Alan drove him home and they didn't talk much. That silence wasn't one of their usual comfortable interludes. It felt loaded with uncertainty and things that both of them wanted to say, but neither of them could.

How did you tell someone that you'd only known for a single day, that they'd made your life infinitely better just by existing? How could you admit that you didn't want to go home because you already couldn't stand the thought of being away from them? Craig didn't love Alan, he hadn't known him long enough, but he *wanted* to love him. It would be the easiest thing in the world to fall in love with a man as amazing as Alan.

Like the gentleman he'd been for most of their time together, Alan held his hand and walked him to his door.

Alan—typical tactile Alan—reached out and cupped Craig's cheek and Craig let himself melt into the touch. "When can I see you again?"

"Whenever you want." Craig smiled. "I'm off work by six each night."

Alan smiled and leaned in a little closer. "Dinner tomorrow night?"

"I'd like that." Craig couldn't keep the smile from his face.

"Wonderful. I'll pick you up here at eight, then."

"Sounds great."

Craig's pulse sped up and his world tilted on its axis when Alan leaned in and kissed him. It started out slow and sweet. His lips brushed against Craig's all smooth and soft before Alan melted into Craig. He pulled him close and sighed and parted Craig's lips with his tongue. Craig turned to boneless mush in Alan's arms. He wrapped his arms around Alan's neck and held on tight as Alan kissed him.

By the time he pulled away, Alan was breathless and panting. Craig could feel his rock-solid erection press against him and he wanted nothing more than to tug Alan into his apartment and take care of it, but he settled for another toe curling kiss instead. Alan explored every bit of Craig's mouth with his tongue. When they parted Alan rested his forehead against Craig's with a sigh.

"I've been wanting to do that since I first saw you."

"It was worth waiting for."

6
Alan

ALAN THOUGHT OF DRIVING home, but he found himself near the club and walking into The Dragon's Den instead. He needed someone to talk to about the last twenty-four hours and he thought Steve the perfect person. He'd known Alan the longest and he knew what he'd been through with Mike, and what he went through when Mike left him.

Alan had barely sat down when Steve took the seat across from him.

Steve put his arms on the table and leaned in. "Who was that sweet little hottie you had here last night?"

Alan laughed in spite of hating the fact that Steve noticed Craig. Craig was absolutely off limits. Besides, he was all wrong for Steve who liked things rough and dirty. Craig's soft sweetness would not match well with Steve. "His name is Craig."

Steve whistled. "Craig is cute. What's he doing with an old fart like you?"

"Hey. Who are you calling old? You're two and a half months older than me."

"Is he even legal?" Steve asked with a grin as he waved one of his waiters over.

"He's twenty-three."

"Ah, so he's barely legal." Steve winked and turned to his waiter, a strapping young man who had yet to win Steve over with his charms. Steve didn't care if his staff fucked each other, but he knew that fucking his staff was a bad idea. Alan had to hand it to the kid though, he'd been there for two years and was still trying to win his friend over.

Steve looked at him as the waiter swept away to get the bottle of wine Steve ordered for them. Finished with ribbing his friend, Steve turned serious. "I take it you met him at the club."

"I spotted him the minute he walked in."

Steve rolled his eyes. "Of course you did. He's exactly your type."

Alan raised an eyebrow. "My type?"

Steve grinned. "Please, Alan, I watched the two of you together. The kid seems quite sweet and vulnerable. Admit it, him and his big brown puppy dog eyes trip all your triggers."

"If I admit that I like him, will that make you stop saying stupid shit?"

Steve leaned back, and he looked at Alan. He crossed his arms over his chest and stared at him. The waiter chose that moment to appear with a soda for Alan and the wine Steve ordered. He poured Steve a glass while Steve burned holes into Alan's brain with a knowing look.

When the waiter left Alan reached for his drink. "How much do you like this kid?"

Alan wasn't quite sure how to answer that at first, so he took a big swallow of his soda. "I like him enough to ask you if I like him too much." His cheeks burned as he half spoke half whispered his admission.

"Shit, you really do like him."

"Is that fucked up? I met him last night and while I won't go into detail, we had an amazing time together."

"Jesus fuck. I know that look. You want to offer him a contract, don't you?" When Alan didn't immediately respond Steve's eyes widened.

Alan dropped his gaze. If he refused to answer, it was still and admission that yes, he'd thought about offering a contract to the sweet little sub, but he couldn't bring himself to confirm or deny. Which was exactly the reason he sat there. He needed to know if he was losing his mind.

Steve grabbed his glass of wine and drained half. "For the record, I think you're absolutely insane, but you always did go about things in your own weird way. You never really were one to follow the pack. So, what is it about this kid that has you all twisted up in knots?"

Alan took a deep breath, another drink and tried to gather his thoughts in a way that would make sense to, well, anyone, because he couldn't make sense of it himself.

"Okay, tell me how the two of you met. I know you met in the club. Elaborate."

"I saw him when he walked in." Alan laughed a little. "I noticed him because he was the only other fully dressed person in the place. I watched him for a bit. He went to the bar. He looked nervous and more than a little uncomfortable. It looked like he was going to jump into the scene, then Tim targeted him."

Steve's eyebrows rose so high they would've touched his hairline had he not been completely bald. "Tim? Paul's boy?"

"Yeah. Craig went ten shades whiter when Tim approached him. I didn't really know what was going on, but the next thing I know, Paul put one of his big bear paws on Craig's shoulder to stop him from walking away and Craig swatted it off."

"Holy shit. Kid's got balls."

"I got there just as Paul grabbed him by the arm."

"Shit. What'd you do? Please tell me you punched him."

"No. But one wrong move and his membership is toast. I don't give a shit if I have to invent a reason, I'll cut him loose." Alan told him the rest of the story, about how he'd ordered Craig down to his knees and then dealt with Paul and Tim. He told him about taking Craig into his office and all the other things they did that night. If Steve was going to help him get his head on straight, he had to have all the details.

"So. Tell me I'm crazy. Tell me that I'm absolutely insane."

Steve didn't miss a beat. "You're totally nuts."

Alan's shoulders sagged a little, and he stared into his empty glass. Before he could decide if he was happy about Steve agreeing with him or not, Steve laughed.

"Alan, it's obvious that you're totally taken with the kid, so what's holding you back? I've never known you to hesitate like this. Once you decide you want something you lock onto it like a goddamned heat-seeking-missile. What's the deal?"

"All I can think about is how great I feel when I'm with him and how shitty I feel when I'm not. I dropped him off an hour ago, Steve, and it's all I can do not to drive back over there and beg him to come home with me again."

"So?"

"So?" Alan repeated, incredulously.

"It's obvious that you like the guy. A bit of obsession to begin with is natural. It's like when you get a shiny new toy for Christmas and you want to play with it all day every day. That's the first flush of lust, my friend."

"How can I tell if it's more than that?" Alan's heart raced. He desperately wanted it to be more than lust. There was something about Craig that was addictive.

Steve grabbed the bottle of wine and topped up his glass. "When the novelty wears off and you still want your toy with you all the time, even if you don't play quite as often, and you can't bear to think what would happen if you were to suddenly lose your toy, then you're probably in love." Steve swirled his wine, then looked at Alan with a raised eyebrow. "But you should know all this. You and Mike were together for a long time."

"That was different." Alan snatched the napkin off the table so he'd have something to fidget with.

"How?"

"Because when I met Mike we were both young and stupid. We played hard and fell harder and by the time I realized that Mike was probably never really right for me to begin with, he'd already been gone for two years."

Steve's face fell. "He really did a number on you, huh?"

Alan could only nod. The pain wasn't fresh anymore, but he could still feel the wound. On nights like tonight, when he felt completely unsure of everything, including himself, it made him aware of how much Mike had hurt him. Needy, Mike had called him. Needy and clingy. According to Mike, Alan possessed ample amounts of both of those traits. He'd hoped Alan would grow into his big-bad Dom over the years, and felt bitter disappointment when it didn't happen. Truth be told, Alan was never a badass, not the way Mike wanted, but he'd done his best to be what Mike needed. It wasn't enough. But Craig seemed to relish the things that Mike hated. Craig responded to Alan's tactile nature.

"Alan?" Steve said after a long silence. The gentle tone caused Alan to tense. Steve was only gentle if he knew he was about to be a complete bastard. He thought it softened the blow, but it really made it worse. If he was a cocky bastard, Alan might feel justified in punching him in the mouth, but when he was *nice*, it meant that he was looking out for Alan and if he punched Steve in the mouth it would make Alan the asshole. "Is it possible that you see this kid and think, gee, I went through the same damned thing, and you want to make it better for him because you still haven't found a way to make it better for yourself?"

Alan's hand tightened on the napkin and his teeth ground together. He hadn't considered that possibility. The room spun, and Alan's stomach lurched. No. His feelings for Craig were real. They were new and scared the life out of Alan. Maybe that's how he knew they were real. Because if they weren't he wouldn't feel half as terrified as he did.

He forced his hand to relax and dropped the napkin on the table. "No." He said with a confidence that shocked him. "That's not it at all. This isn't some broken sub that the big all-knowing Dom is riding to the rescue of… except for last night. Craig doesn't need to be rescued and he's not broken. He went to my club last night because he was ready to move on and I noticed him because so am I."

Steve grinned and plucked his wine glass off the table. "I have to get back to running this place or it's all going to fall down around me, but I'm glad you came, Alan." He raised his glass. "To you and the kid, may Cupid shoot your asses with a matching set of arrows. You deserve all the happiness you can get."

Alan shook his head and stifled a smile. "Get back to work, slacker."

The pair stood and Steve tugged Alan into a bone crushing hug. "Seriously, Alan. If you want the kid, go for it."

Alan clapped him on the back and pulled away. "Only if you stop calling him *the kid.* His name is Craig."

Steve winked. "No promises."

Instead of going home, Alan went to the club and slipped into his office. He locked the door behind him to avoid being disturbed. He poured himself a glass of water and drank it, all the while he stared at the filing cabinet in the corner. When his water was gone, he went to the cabinet, opened the top drawer and pulled out a blank contract. He rolled it up, slipped out of the club and went home. Waiting until eight o'clock the next night would be murder.

7
Craig

CRAIG BROUGHT HIS HAND to his lips and touched them. He hadn't stopped smiling since Alan left a few minutes ago. He doubted that he'd stop any time soon. Craig just entered the living room, still daydreaming about Alan when he heard a knock at his door.

His heart fluttered in his chest. Maybe it was Alan. Maybe two kisses weren't enough. Craig certainly felt that way. He could've spent hours doing nothing but laying in Alan's arms, kissing him until they were both senseless.

Craig hurried to his door and flung it open, his bright smile dimmed when he saw it was his neighbor. Craig's shoulders drooped, and he ran a hand through his hair. "Oh, hey Everett. What can I do for you?" Hands stuffed in his pockets, Everett rocked back and forth on the balls of his feet. When not filming, Everett was a quiet, laid back guy. Craig met him in the hallway a few times and they struck up a friendship.

They often sought the other out and somehow, they started sharing a bottle of wine every so often and would talk about everything. Everett's friendship had come to mean a lot to Craig.

"There was a guy here looking for you today." Craig stepped aside and motioned for Everett to come in.

"A guy?"

"Yeah, some moron let him past the security doors. He was in the hallway, banging on your door and yelling at you to open up."

Craig leaned against the wall for support. "Did you see him? What did he look like?"

"Um . . . a little taller than you, short black hair."

Craig's stomach lurched, and he swallowed a rush of bile. "That sounds like Tim."

Everett's eyes widened. "The guy who dumped you? What was he doing here?"

Craig laughed, and it came out strained and uneasy. He suddenly felt off kilter. "That's a good question. I moved here after we broke up, he shouldn't know where I am." Craig wrapped his arms around himself and felt his chest tighten. "Did he say what he wanted?"

"No. I told him you weren't home." Everett narrowed his eyes and gave Craig a curious look. "You stayed out all night, didn't you?"

Craig's cheeks heated, and he managed a nod. Alan. God, what he wouldn't give to be able to crawl onto his lap and melt into his arms at that very moment. "I wonder how Tim knew where I lived? That's creepy." Craig's skin crawled.

There was a time when he would've welcomed the thought of Tim showing up at his door. He used to imagine the euphoria he'd feel if Tim showed up, knocked and threw himself on his knees, begging for forgiveness. But Craig grew out of that daydream fast. Then the idea of seeing Tim only enraged and sickened him, so he moved.

"I have to get home, I have a ton of footage to edit, but if you need anything I'm here, okay."

Craig nodded and cracked a weak smile. "Thanks for letting me know, Everett. We'll catch up soon, okay?"

Everett nodded and let himself out. Craig's knees refused to hold his weight any longer and he sank to the floor. He didn't like the creepy-crawly feeling that made his skin itch. There were too many questions and Craig didn't like not having the answers. Why after all this time did Tim choose today to seek him out? How did Tim know where he lived? What would Alan think of Tim showing up at his house?

Craig dropped his head to his knees and forced himself to take a few deep breaths. There was no sense in dwelling on any of it. Stewing and worrying weren't going to give him any of the answers he was looking for.

A shower didn't wash off the creeped-out feeling and watching TV didn't distract him from trying to find answers for the questions that plagued him and none of it helped him get any sleep. By the time morning rolled around Craig felt wrecked. He'd barely slept, but other than the night with Alan, sleepless nights were the norm.

He arrived at work on time with his second extra large coffee half gone. He ditched it in the staff room, took a perfunctory glance in the mirror and decided that he looked no worse than he did most days.

Work provided a welcome distraction. There was always a problem to solve and a customer to please and the pettiness of some of their problems was welcome. At least insignificant problems like a room that faces the wrong direction, or a pillow that's not fluffy enough had easy solutions.

It was almost two in the afternoon and Craig was about to slip into the back for a break. He'd taken a bottle of champagne to a frequent flyer in one of the suites to apologize for some sort of tragic linen mix-up that shorted them a few towels or something, Craig couldn't quite remember. His mind was a puddle of goo and all he could think about was the fact that he had six more hours to wait until he got to see Alan again.

Craig got halfway through the lobby when he heard his name. He turned and wasn't at all shocked to see Tim there. Craig stormed over to Tim, righteous indignation fuelled the volcanic anger that stewed in him. "What are you doing here? And were you at my apartment yesterday? How do you even know where I live? Do you know how creepy that is?"

Tim raised his hands. "Woah, there, buddy, calm down."

Craig's cheeks flamed, and he crossed his arms in front of himself. "I will not calm down. You have ten seconds to tell me what the hell you're doing here."

"I wanted to see you. I need to talk to you, to explain some things."

Craig shook his head. "I don't give a shit, Tim. Do you know why I went to the club the other night?" He didn't give Tim a chance to answer. "Because I'm over you. I moved on.

You left me. You walked away. You don't get to come here a year and a half later to explain anything to me. Whatever forgiveness you're looking for, you'll have to live without it because I don't forgive you and I won't. Now leave."

"Craig, please. Five minutes, that's all I want."

Craig shook his head. Tim seemed perfect on paper. College grad, good job, nice parents who didn't care that he was gay. He excelled at talking with people and getting his own way. Tim was charming, but Craig wasn't going to fall for any of it and didn't want to hear anything he had to say.

"Leave."

Tim furrowed his brow and had the decency to look annoyed instead of hard done by. "Come on, Craig, please."

Craig pulled his phone from his pocket and sent a text. God how he loved technology at times like this. "You have ten seconds."

"Five minutes, please. Okay, two, two minutes."

"There a problem here?" One of two very large men in hotel uniforms appeared seemingly out of nowhere and Craig tucked his phone back in his pocket. He watched Tim turn his head and realize he was eye-to-chest with a hotel security guard.

"No. Please, Craig. You don't understand, I made a mistake." Tim reached for Craig, but Craig stepped back.

"This man is causing a scene. He's not a guest and should be escorted off the premises. If he gives you any trouble, call the police." With a final thought, Craig pulled his phone out of his pocket and took a picture of Tim. "I'll send you this picture, I want him banned for life. If he comes back here, have him arrested."

Craig turned on his heel and left. He ignored Tim's angry shouts and disappeared into the back. He sank down onto a couch in the staff room and buried his face into his shaking hands. He wanted to yell, scream and throw things. None of this felt fair. It had to be some sort of cosmic joke, the minute he was ready to move on, Tim was suddenly everywhere and demanding attention.

His phone pinged in his pocket and he almost ignored it, but he reluctantly pulled it out and looked at the screen. Not Tim, or work or anyone else, it was Alan. Can't wait to see you. Craig shot a text back to him. He wasn't going to wait and pretend he didn't want to reply right away or play some sort of other head game. Truthfully, he couldn't make himself wait if he tried, he liked Alan too much. I can't wait to see you, either.

With a renewed vigour, Craig pried himself off the couch and threw himself into his job. The guys from security came to check on him. Craig had been at the hotel so long everyone knew him, and they all looked out for him. He sometimes felt like the hotel pet. His assurances that he was fine got accepted, if not believed and he was ecstatic when his shift ended so he could escape the ever repeated question, *are you okay?* If he'd known the answer he might not have been so annoyed by the question.

Alan picked him up at his door at five minutes to eight. He dressed down in pair of dark blue jeans and a dark grey polo shirt. He greeted Craig by stepping in close to him. Alan put a hand on his waist and another on the side of Craig's face and pulled him into an agonizingly gentle kiss.

It was just what Craig needed. He let himself melt into

Alan's arms. He wound his arms around Alan's waist and let his hands roam up Alan's back. Alan's soft kiss was hot and Craig let out a sigh when it ended.

"Hi," Alan said. "Ready to go?"

"Or we could stay here and do that all night." Craig gave into the urge to bury himself against Alan's chest. After the hellish night and then the scene with Tim at work earlier, Alan was exactly what he needed.

"Come on. We'll grab some dinner and you can tell me all about your day."

Halfway to the car Alan glanced at Craig.

"Everything okay? You look stressed."

"That obvious?"

Alan nodded. "You're completely tense. Which means either you're not as excited about tonight as I thought you were, or there's something else on your mind."

"Definitely the second one."

When they stopped beside the car, Alan opened the passenger door for Craig. "If you'd like, we could get something to go and take it back to my place. We can relax and maybe you can tell me what's troubling you."

Craig's dismal mood lifted a little. "That sounds fantastic." On impulse he rose up on his tiptoes and kissed Alan on the cheek. Going back to Alan's place had been on Craig's mind all day long, when he wasn't thinking about Tim. He also knew that Alan would want him to talk about what was bothering him and he had little desire to sit in a restaurant and gossip about his life.

Craig was back in Alan's home before some of his tension

started to ease. They'd stopped at a little Chinese place on the way and grabbed enough food to feed an army. He discovered that Alan hadn't tried many of Craig's favorite dishes.

"I still can't believe you've only ever eaten Chow Mein and Chop Suey." Craig said as he helped Alan unpack the food and arrange it on the coffee table. Craig had jumped at the offer to eat in the living room. As far as first dates went, it really didn't get better than Alan, a table full of food and the prospect of curling up in his arms afterward.

"What can I say?" Alan shrugged as he took a seat on the sofa. "I guess I'm not that adventurous."

"Said the dommy owner of a kink club to the sub holding a container of Kung Pow Chicken."

Alan's musical laughter lifted his spirit and even better was the ruffle of his fingers through Craig's hair. "How about you sit here?" Alan's eyes flashed down to the empty space at his feet.

Craig didn't hesitate. He knelt by Alan's feet. He didn't realize how much he needed it until Alan's fingers carded through his hair again. More of the tension that had built up over the course of the day left. His shoulders loosened, and he took a deep breath. Craig leaned into Alan's touch. He could get used to this. Quiet dinners with Alan, kneeling at his feet, being taken care of. It was perfect.

Alan grabbed a container and showed it to Craig. "What are these?"

"Deep fried prawns." He laughed when Alan wrinkled his nose. "Don't knock it until you try it."

Alan rolled his eyes but plucked a prawn out of the box.

"You sound like Steve." He bit the prawn in half. "Hmmm. Not bad. Here, you try."

Alan held the prawn out and Craig's dick did a happy dance with his heart. *Oh, fuck yes.* He leaned in and carefully took the rest of the prawn from Alan's fingers. His lips didn't touch Alan's fingers, but it didn't matter, the jolt of electricity zapped them both. Craig looked up at Alan. Alan smiled and stroked a finger down Craig's cheek.

"Tell me what happened today."

Craig did his best to curb his imagination, but everything Alan did convinced him that he'd be the perfect Daddy. *Tell me what happened today, Baby,* Alan would command. Craig would kiss him on the cheek, or snuggle in close, and he'd tell his Daddy all about it.

Craig took a deep breath, and reached for a container and a set of chopsticks. He would've liked it if Alan fed him all night long, but he needed something to occupy his hands. "After you dropped me off last night, my friend Everett came to see me. He lives in the apartment across the hall from mine and works from home. He wanted me to know that there was a guy pounding on my door yesterday. Based on Everett's description and what happened at work today, I think it was Tim."

"What happened at work?"

"Tim came to see me. He caused a scene in the lobby and I had security throw him out."

Alan didn't speak for a moment. Then the questions came, "What did he want? Did he say?"

Craig frowned and stared at his container of food as he realized his appetite had vanished. It didn't shock him, he never could eat when upset. He put the container back on the table. "He wanted to talk to me. He begged me for a few minutes of my time." Craig frowned. "He said he made a mistake." Craig scoffed. "Fine time to realize that, a year and a half after he up and left me."

"Do you think he was there to try and win you back?" Alan's voice sounded strained and unsure, like the man feared Craig would run back into Tim's arms if Tim said he was sorry.

Craig shrugged. "I don't know what Tim wants and I really don't care. I don't want to see him, and I certainly don't want to get back together."

Alan rested a hand on Craig's shoulder and he leaned into the touch. "I'm sorry your day was rough."

Craig sighed. "I'm annoyed. I wasn't good enough to talk to when he dumped me, and I was frantically trying to reach him, but I'm good enough to talk to now when I'm finally moving on."

"Maybe seeing you at the club affected him in some way."

"I don't care." Craig got angry. He'd spent so much time and energy trying to move on and *now* all of a sudden Tim wanted to talk. He hadn't been good enough for the other man when they were together, nor important enough to Tim when he left to give Craig a proper explanation. "I don't care if he suddenly feels the need for my forgiveness or something, he has no right to show up at my job, or my home. I don't even know how he knows where I live."

Alan raked his fingers through Craig's hair and Craig closed his eyes. He leaned into Alan and savoured the gentle touch. "He didn't know where you live?"

"At first I stayed in the apartment we had together. It was all I had left of him, at first. But it didn't even feel like home anymore, not without Tim. I moved months ago. The rent is a little more, but the building is nicer, and it doesn't come with baggage and talking walls."

"Talking walls?"

Craig laughed. "You know how it is when you're used to spending time with someone in a specific location and they're not there anymore, you look around and see flashes of what your life used to be like. I like my new place because there aren't any memories associated with Tim." Craig unclenched his fists and took a deep breath. "He ruined it you know. When I got home from work today, I could almost *see* him in my hallway, banging on my door, yelling my name."

"Do you think he wants you back?" Alan asked again.

"I don't care what Tim wants. I care about what I want." Craig turned his head and looked up at Alan. "I care about what you want."

Craig couldn't read Alan's expression. A mixture of apprehension, excitement, and maybe even tenderness, it was gone as soon as it appeared. The man was far too good at schooling his expressions. Alan reached over and grabbed an envelope off the side table. He handed it to Craig, who willed his hands not to shake as he took it.

"What's this?"

"It's what I want."

8
Alan

HE WATCHED CRAIG'S HANDS tremble as he opened the envelope and removed its contents. Alan found himself wishing he drank. Some alcoholic fortification would help quell the nerves that crashed through him in sickening waves. He wanted to bury his face in his hands, hide and not watch Craig's face while he searched every little twitch for the answers the boy's mouth wasn't giving him. But as much as he didn't want to watch, couldn't bear to watch, he also couldn't bear to look away.

"It's a contract. A trial contract. Three months."

Craig didn't say anything. He stared down at the pages in his hands, which thankfully stopped trembling, but his expression remained blank.

He turned his head and looked up at Alan. "You had this ready, sitting there, waiting for me."

Alan nodded. He got the sense that Craig was working

through something in his head and didn't want to speak until he got it out, in case it sidetracked him. He wanted to understand Craig's thoughts and feelings.

"You were going to offer me a contract tonight, even before the Tim thing. So, this isn't some jealous Dom thing?"

Alan smiled and resisted the urge to grab Craig and kiss him. "No, it's not a jealous Dom thing. I want this. I want you. I want to get to know you in all the ways there is to know you. I want to know what your favorite Chinese foods taste like and I want to know what shows you watch and I want to know what you look like bound and begging and kneeling at my feet."

Craig moaned. "You're killing me." He looked down at the contract and grinned. By the time Craig had given the contract a quick perusal his smile had faltered.

"What is it?"

Craig closed the contract and looked at it. Alan watched as his hand smoothed over the front of it, as if he were still wondering if it was real.

"What if the kind of thing I wanted isn't in here?"

"We'd talk about it, of course. Before we do anything, we have to agree on it, always. If there's something you want or need, you should tell me so we can discuss it."

Craig stayed silent for a long time. Alan could tell he was nervous. He raked his fingers through Craig's hair over and over. He hated seeing Craig tied up in so many knots. "What is it? I'm a Dom, Craig, there's nothing you can ask for that I'm going to find shocking."

"It's just . . . when Tim left . . . I spent a lot of time wondering what went wrong. He was always so aggressive, you know. He always wanted to do the extreme things. Sounding. Flogging. Caning. He wanted me to like all of that, but I don't. What I really wanted was to have someone to take care of me."

"Take care of you how? What do you need, Craig?"

Craig slowly turned his head and looked up at Alan. His brown eyes shimmered with apprehension. "A Daddy." Craig's voice was thin and barely audible. Alan heard the quiver of fear in it.

Alan cupped Craig's cheeks with his hands. He smoothed his thumbs over Craig's cheekbones and smiled at him. "I'd be honored to take care of you."

Alan almost couldn't believe his ears. He'd wanted this so much, and thought it was too much to hope for it, but now it was here. He'd offered Craig a contract and he hadn't said no. "I should let you know right now that I'm not looking for a full-time boy. I want to be more than just your Daddy."

Craig's cheeks turned the sexiest shade of pink he'd ever seen, and he flipped the contract open to the first page. "Good. Because I want to be more than just your boy. I love being taken care of, and I love having a Dom, but I want to do regular boyfriend things, too." Craig's cheeks flushed.

"Okay, Little One, take a look at the contract. I need to know everything you like and don't like and everything you're not sure of. I expect complete honesty, do you understand?"

"Yes . . . Daddy."

Fuck. He didn't expect this, but it was better than anything he'd imagined. Alan lost his appetite in the excitement, but he picked away at a container of dry garlic pork while Craig perused the contract. After a few silent moments that switched between tense and awkward, then Craig put the contract in his lap and looked up at Alan. His eyes harboured a look of uncertainty that unsettled Alan. He reached for Craig and ran his fingers through his hair.

"What's wrong?"

"Well . . . I don't really have a ton of experience. Besides my hard limits and the few things I know I like . . . I don't really know about any of that other stuff. I know what it is, don't get me wrong, but I don't know if I like any of it, or if I will like any of it. Tim wasn't experienced enough to try a lot of the things on this list."

Alan hated watching Craig struggle like this. On one hand, it was endearing. He was absolutely gorgeous when he was shy, but Alan didn't care much for the tremor of fear in Craig's voice, so he did his best to alleviate his worries.

"It's okay, Little One. I'm the dommy owner of a kink club and you're a sweet little sub who I can't wait to play with. Inexperience is never a bad thing. Everyone at one time or another was new to this. There's nothing to be embarrassed about."

"That sounds good in theory, but then I remember that I've been in your club, I've seen what goes on there and . . ."

Craig didn't finish his sentence. That kind of behaviour would change when Alan became his Dom, but he'd let it slide for now. Craig was unsure of himself and it was Alan's job to put his fears to rest.

He raked his fingers through Craig's hair. Craig leaned into his touch and Alan's cock stiffened in his pants. The boy was gorgeous. "Sweetheart, you have nothing to be embarrassed about. Your inexperience is a delight."

Something that looked a little like hope shone on Craig's face. "Really?"

Alan nodded and slid his fingertips along Craig's jaw until he was cupping his chin. "It means that we get to explore all kinds of things together. We'll go slow and you never, ever have to do anything you don't want to do. That's why this contract is so important. Communication is the most important thing in a relationship like this. Well, that and a healthy appetite for kink."

"So, if I say I don't want to do something, we don't have to do it, no matter what it is?"

Alan wanted to frown at the look of near terror on Craig's face, but he schooled his expression. "Of course not. That's why we're talking about limits now, and that's why there are safe words for later. If you say something is off limits, it's off limits. We can always discuss limits again in the future, and you might change your mind about certain things, and you might not."

"And you won't be mad if I don't want to do certain things?"

Now Alan did frown. "Why would I be mad? This is supposed to equally enjoyable for both of us. I couldn't enjoy myself knowing that you were honestly uncomfortable with something."

"So, if I said that I didn't want to be put on display . . . or that I didn't want to like . . . play . . . at your club . . . in any way . . . or that I don't like pain . . ."

"I would never force you to do anything you weren't comfortable with. Ever."

"And if I do try something and I use my safe word . . . what happens then?"

Alan really didn't like the road this line of questioning was going down. Alarm bells started to ring in his head and he wondered what kind of training he'd received and what kind of Dom Tim had been. "We stop. Immediately and without repercussion."

Alan took a deep breath. He warred with the idea of asking about his experiences with Tim, but decided that Craig would open up more when he was ready. "If you don't want to play at the club, that's more than okay with me. You don't even have to call me Daddy or Sir there if you don't want to. I'm not going to be at all disappointed if you want to keep our private life private. If you want this to be kept strictly between us, I'm fine with that."

"You are?" Craig's uncertainty was absolutely killing him.

Alan nodded. "How about you bring that contract up here and we'll finish looking it over together."

Craig wasted no time climbing onto the couch and into Alan's lap. Craig rested his head against Alan's shoulder and he was relieved to feel some of the tension leave the young man.

Craig's hard limits weren't a complete surprise. Alan always guessed that Craig wasn't going to be into the more extreme scenes in BDSM. There was a time when the idea of having a sub who didn't want to be flogged and whipped into oblivion might not have been appealing to Alan, then memories of their first scene together flooded Alan. Craig was so responsive to all of Alan's gentle touches. Alan remembered how much he'd enjoyed being with Craig and taking care of him. Craig wasn't into pain. Spanking was fine, but he didn't like much else. Alan could live with that. Exhibitionism was up in the air. He said it might be fun, but he admitted that it scared the pants off him to think about it too much. He liked bondage and admitted that he'd never thought much about humiliation play. Based on the results of their talk, Alan knew that sensory play would be one of his favorite things to do with Craig.

Despite how infrequently he'd had to do it, contract talks were never Alan's favorite thing to do, and he was glad when they were done. With a flourish, Craig scrawled his name on the bottom. Alan added his own, then set it aside.

"So..." Craig fidgeted in Alan's lap a little. "How exactly does this boyfriend slash Daddy and boy thing work for us? Like...do I call you Daddy all the time now?"

"Well, how do you want it to work?" Alan wrapped his arms around Craig and pressed a kiss to the top of his head.

"I liked calling you Sir, and I really like calling you Daddy, but I also like being us, and I think I'd like to start out slow, like you said, but...this is going to sound stupid."

"Your feelings and your thoughts are never stupid."

Craig took a deep breath. "When Tim and I discovered BDSM, it was like a switch flipped in his head and it was all he wanted to do. He wanted every intimate thing between us to be a scene. He didn't want to shower with me anymore unless he could put me on my knees and use me. He didn't want to fuck me anymore unless he could tie me up. Everything we did got more and more intense." Craig frowned. "He got really obsessed for a while. He must have realized he was getting too extreme for me because a few months before he left, he suddenly backed off."

Alan could guess why, and he hated the idea of telling Craig about Tim's unfaithfulness, but he deserved to know, especially if Tim continued harassing him. Alan wanted to make sure that Craig knew exactly what Tim had been up to in those last few months of their relationship. Maybe it was selfish, but Alan couldn't stand the thought of Tim winning Craig back, if that was his plan. Sure, him and Craig had amazing chemistry, but Craig and Tim had history.

"Craig, there's something you should know about Tim." Alan paused and when Craig didn't object to Alan relaying the information he continued. "He's been a member of my club for two years."

Craig remained silent and Alan could practically feel his heart fall. Even though him and Tim hadn't been together in a long time, sometimes old betrayal left fresh wounds. But Craig deserved to know, so he continued.

"He came in one night about two years ago. Paul had his sights set on Tim from the moment he walked in the door. Paul is a Dom, and while Tim might have been the Dom in your relationship, he joined the club as a sub and made it known that he liked to switch on occasion, which is right up Paul's alley. They did a few scenes together before signing a temporary contract. If I remember correctly, Tim left you around the same time that Paul offered him a permanent contract."

Alan held Craig tighter and pressed a kiss to his head. "I'm sorry, Sweetheart." Alan was glad when the endearment didn't make Craig flinch, but he wasn't pleased with his silence. "Are you mad at me? Should I not have told you?"

Craig shook his head and wiped his face. "No. I'm glad you told me." His voice warbled, and Alan was sorry that he'd told him. Maybe he should've kept the information to himself, because now Craig was crying, and Alan felt responsible.

Craig turned in Alan's arms and buried his face into Alan's chest. Alan held him as a stream of tears fell. Craig was heartbreakingly silent, and Alan felt stupid and mean and selfish for telling him.

"I don't even know why I'm crying. He's been gone for so long, and I don't even like him anymore, and I like you now, and it's stupid to feel hurt over this, but fuck, Alan. He said that he wasn't what I needed when this whole time it was me . . . I wasn't what he needed. I wasn't enough for a wannabe Dom who was really a sub or a switch or who the fuck cares. How can I be enough for you if I wasn't enough for him?"

Tears pricked at the corner of Alan's eyes. He cradled Craig against him. "Oh, Sweetheart. I'm sorry I told you. I don't want you to feel this way. I don't want you to feel like you're not enough for me. Remember when I talked about all the subs who only want hardcore scenes and nothing more from me, *those* subs weren't enough. I don't want someone who will let me do anything to them. I want someone like you, who still wants his own life and his own passions and who wants a real relationship and who likes to play, but needs me to take care of him. I don't want to always have to be the big bad Dom. I was him for so many years. Mike wanted the big bad dom. Mike was like Tim, I suppose. He wanted the hardcore stuff, and yeah, that was all well and good and I loved being what he needed, but he never wanted me to take care of him. He called me needy and clingy. For the past while I haven't been a dom. I've been Alan, and I really, really like being Alan. I also really like being the guy who gets to take care of you." Alan kissed Craig's head again. "Do you understand?"

Craig snuggled closer and his tears seemed to have stopped. His breathing evened out a little more before he finally spoke. "I'm not sorry you told me, Alan. And… yeah, I really do understand what you mean."

"Stay with me tonight? I liked waking up to you."

"I'll stay."

9

Craig

EMBARRASSMENT LINGERED WHEN ALAN brought him a cloth to wipe his tear stained face with. Alan sat back down next to him as Craig mopped his face. "This is probably the strangest first date ever."

Alan rubbed Craig's back and Craig shut his eyes. He enjoyed the way Alan always wanted to touch him, he doubted he'd ever get enough.

"It's definitely a night I'm going to remember."

Craig turned his head and cocked an eyebrow at Alan. "Why? Going to take your new sub out for a spin? Tie him up and flog up and see if he'll come?" Craig laughed and was relieved when Alan shook his head.

"No. I'm going to take my new boyfriend up to my bed and I'm going to kiss him until we pass out. And then, in the morning, I'm going to kiss him some more, but only for a little while, because I have to get him to work on time."

Craig stood up and started to gather the containers of food off the coffee table. "Then I guess we should clean this up, so we can get on with our plans."

Alan laughed, and rose to help him. "Eager, are we?"

Craig sighed and looked at Alan from the corner of his eye. "Truthfully, I've been looking forward to being with you all day long." Craig stilled. "Do you think it's weird for us to move this fast? We just met and we've already like . . . crossed certain lines and signed a Dom/sub sex contract. We've established that you're willing to be my Daddy and my boyfriend. Does it bother you at all?"

Alan arched an eyebrow. "Does it bother you?"

"It feels like it *should* bother me. I don't think it's fast, but then I think of what other people will think, or how they'd see it and it makes me wonder if we did move really fast."

Alan walked up to Craig and leaned in. He kissed him sweetly on the lips, then winked at him when he pulled away. "I think we're moving at the exact pace we've decided is right for us and I think anyone who isn't us doesn't get to voice an opinion about our relationship, not one that matters."

"Gah." Craig exhaled and then laughed. "Are you the perfect boyfriend or something?"

That made Alan laugh as they headed for the kitchen. "I'm not the perfect boyfriend. I'm sometimes jealous and always possessive and I'll probably forget an anniversary at one point or another."

Craig liked the idea that Alan was already thinking of being with him long enough to have an anniversary with him, let alone forget about one. Craig watched Alan as he put all the various containers in the fridge. Contract talk over Chinese food hadn't really been what Craig had expected to happen, not that he was complaining, but every time he thought he had his mind wrapped around everything, he'd think of another question.

"Hey, won't the other Dom's mind if you bring your boyfriend to the club, who is your sub sometimes, but not at the club? Won't that cause a problem?"

Alan shut the fridge and pulled Craig into his arms. "Why would it? It's my club. It's a safe space for everyone, and everyone includes you."

"How'd you come to own a kink club anyway?"

"Well, it's a long story." Alan tugged Craig toward the stairs. "It really wasn't my idea, but the opportunity came up. I'd recently come into some money and Mike really wanted to be a partner, so he got a loan to cover half. It wasn't what I really wanted to do, but I was in a strange place in my life and I didn't really know what I did want to do, and I figured this would be better than nothing."

"What do you mean you were in a strange place?" Craig asked as Alan led them into the bedroom.

Alan's fingers tugged at the bottom of Craig's shirt. "Lift your arms, Sweetheart."

Craig obeyed and stood still while Alan pushed the shirt up his body and gently removed it. Craig melted into Alan's touch as he ran his hands down Craig's bare back. Then Alan wrapped his arms around Craig's waist and nuzzled into the crook of his neck. "My parents had died and the money I eventually invested into the club was from the wrongful death lawsuit that I won."

"Shit. I'm sorry." Craig felt Alan shrug.

"It is what it is."

Craig got the impression that Alan's parents were a subject that was off limits, so he carefully steered the conversation in a different direction. "Why'd you buy Mike out if the club was his idea in the first place?"

"He didn't want it anymore."

"Do you?" Craig popped the button of his pants open and slid out of them. He kept his briefs on and turned to tug Alan's shirt over his head.

"Why wouldn't I want the club?"

Craig shrugged and focused on his shaking fingers as he worked the button of Alan's pants open. "You said that you only invested in it because Mike wanted it and you didn't know what else you were going to do with your life. Seems like you sort of ended up there and stayed there because it's comfortable and familiar."

Craig watched as Alan kicked his pants off. As far as first dates went, this was the weirdest and probably the best one he'd ever been on, Craig thought as Alan tossed the covers back and climbed into bed. He patted the empty space next to him and Craig dutifully climbed in beside him. Alan pulled him in close to him and Craig rested his head on Alan's chest. He slung an arm around Alan's middle.

"You're right, you know. I don't really want the club. I'm not, not-happy there, and it's not something I saw myself doing. It was fine when I had Mike, but Mike's gone and so is my enthusiasm."

Craig's eyes fluttered shut as Alan absent-mindedly stroked

his fingers through Craig's hair. "What would you do if you didn't have the club?"

"I still don't know. I guess that's why I'm still there. It's not like I have an artistic passion I want to pursue. I don't like cooking enough to want to do anything with that particular skill. I got a business degree in college because it made the most sense. It was stupid luck that I ended up being any good at it." Allan nuzzled his nose into Craig's hair and breathed in. "If you weren't at the hotel, what would you want to do?"

"I like my job. I'd still want to be a concierge."

"What do you like about it?"

Craig winced. "Okay, this might sound dumb, but . . . I like feeling useful. I like solving people's mostly first world problems, like not having enough towels or getting a room that faces the wrong view. They have problems that I can fix and most of the time people are genuinely grateful that they got their towels, or their fancy view or that I found them tickets to the concert they wanted to see or that I had a car waiting to take them to the airport."

As Craig rambled on, the feel of Alan's body pressed tightly to his and the sensation of his strong, smooth, hands roaming Craig's body drove him crazy. "I have to admit that this wasn't what I thought we'd be doing after signing that contract."

Alan chuckled and kissed Craig on the top of the head. "Let me guess, you thought I'd immediately order you to kneel, so I could inspect my property."

The words alone woke Craig's dick the rest of the way, but the mental image made him rock solid in seconds. "Something like that." His voice was thick with lust and he didn't try to hide it. He wanted Alan to know how much he wanted him. "What would you have done next?"

One of Alan's hands travelled down Craig's back. Craig resisted the urge to arch his back and seek more contact when Alan's fingers brushed past the crease of his ass. "Well, you were wearing too many clothes, so I probably would've ordered you to stand so I could strip you. Or maybe I'd have made use of my boy and had him suck my cock."

White hot want surged through Craig. He whimpered and Alan's fingers, which had returned to his head and had been delicately toying with his hair, gripped tight.

"Do you like the sound of that, Little One?"

"Yes, Daddy." Craig let his hand slide lower. He couldn't remember the last time he had a cock in his mouth, and nor did he want to. He wanted Alan's cock. "Please, Daddy. Please, can I?" Craig couldn't keep the needy tone out of his voice, but the hint of desperation seemed to please Alan, who kissed Craig on the top of the head.

"Go on. I've been dying to see what that gorgeous mouth of yours is capable of."

Craig knew that eventually Alan would want to have him bound and begging and on his knees. One day soon, Alan would want to tie him up and while the possibility was thrilling, Craig was grateful that they were easing into it. Maybe Alan sensed his apprehension. But there was no room for anything but desire in this moment.

Craig shifted onto his knees and nuzzled into Alan's neck. He kissed the tender flesh below Alan's ear, then placed a series of kisses lower and lower. To see how Alan would react, he nipped gently at Alan's collarbone.

Alan hissed. "Do that again and I'll have to spank you, Boy." His stern words were contrasted by the way he lightly dragged his fingers up Craig's side.

Craig's cock twitched at the vision he got of himself draped over Alan's lap and he toyed with the idea of nipping Alan's collarbone again to ensure that he'd get to feel Alan's hand as it smacked his ass until he was tender and delicate. But he wanted to please Alan more than he wanted that spanking. He continued his journey lower, stopping at each nipple to suck and lave it with his tongue. He kept his teeth to himself, fearing another rebuke from his Daddy. His breath caught. *His Daddy.* He never really thought he'd have that.

Alan flinched when Craig placed a kiss next to his belly button.

"Daddy?" Craig's voice was slightly muffled by Alan's stomach.

"It's okay, Little One," Alan reached down and ruffled Craig's hair. "I'm a little ticklish, that's all."

Craig reached up and brushed a thumb over Alan's nipple as he kissed the same spot, making Alan flinch again.

Craig followed the dark, but barely there, treasure trail down to Alan's eagerly throbbing cock. Alan's fingers slid through Craig's hair. Alan's breath hitched when Craig nuzzled into his thatch of course dark hair, then slicked his tongue up the side of Alan's shaft.

"Oh, fuck yes."

Craig wanted to smile at the easily won praise, but settled

for swirling his tongue around the head of Alan's cock, an action that elicited a low moan. The ink had barely dried on the contract and Craig was already addicted to Alan's sounds.

Normally Craig would shift positions so that he was nestled between Alan's legs. He liked to look up at a guy when he sucked them off. He liked the sense of powerlessness it gave him, knowing that they could, at any moment, take his skull in their hands and fuck his face. Craig continued to lick and lave Alan's cock and Alan's hand caressed the cheek of his ass, his fingers dipped inside the crease and Craig shuddered.

Alan's hand disappeared for a moment, then returned and a spit-slick finger toyed with his hole. Craig whimpered, and he took more of Alan's cock into his mouth. Alan wasn't huge, but he was thick and long. Craig squeezed his eyes shut and tried to relax his gag reflex. Some guys thought it was a huge compliment if you choked on their dick, but it turned others right off, and Craig was too desperate to find out exactly what Alan was going to do with that finger to want to risk it.

Patience was rewarded when Alan's finger teased his entrance, then pressed inside. Spit wasn't the best lube, so it was a bit rough, but that only make Craig's cock thicker. He wrapped a hand around the base of Alan's cock, then sucked him down as far as he could without gagging. He whimpered again when Alan's finger disappeared, cried out when two returned in its place. Alan bucked his hips slightly and Craig focused on teasing Alan's cock with his tongue, and not the frantic need to reach down and grab his own dick and give into the desperate need for friction that clawed at his insides.

Alan kept up a steady, slow pace, that slowly pulled Craig's control apart. He was writhing back on Alan's fingers as he sucked and licked and jacked Alan's thick cock. Then he pulled off and slid his tongue down the length of Alan's shaft. Slowly, he slicked his tongue along Alan's soft sack, then took it gently in his mouth as his hand pumped Alan's cock. This was his favorite part of giving head. Craig loved testicles. He loved having the most delicate part of a man in his mouth. He loved the way the soft skin felt on his tongue and he especially loved the sounds Alan made and the way his body stiffened and twitched.

Alan was fiercely fucking his ass with his fingers, but Craig kept his ministrations slow and gentle.

"Oh, fuck." Alan's hips jerked, and Craig fought the urge to smile as he heard the last bit of Alan's restraint snap. "Fuck. Fuck."

Alan hissed when Craig went back to sucking his cock. As gentle as he was with Alan's sack, he was fierce with his cock. He gripped the base and sucked down to meet his hand. His other hand wandered up Alan's chest and he pinched one of Alan's nipples. Alan's other hand flew to cup the back of Craig's head, but he only rested it there, he didn't push down. Then his hips bucked, and Alan cried out as he shot his load down Craig's throat.

Craig struggled not to gag as the semen shot the back of his throat, and he succeeded, but only barely. Before he could release Alan from his mouth, Alan's fingers slid out of his ass. Craig whimpered and released Alan's cock. He rested his head on Alan's hip and breathed heavily as Alan went back to caressing his ass.

"Please, Daddy. Please."

Craig hissed when Alan gripped a handful of his ass cheek. "Not tonight, Little One."

Craig raised his head and looked at Alan. He didn't even consider arguing with Daddy. If Daddy was satisfied, that's all Craig cared about.

Alan smiled, and warmth surged through Craig as Alan cupped his cheek. "Good boy. I know you're really worked up right now, and I'm proud of you for taking it so well. Come up for a cuddle, okay. You won't be coming tonight, but that doesn't mean I'm not going to reward you at all."

Craig couldn't stop grinning like an idiot as he shifted position and curled into Alan's side. He was still hard as a rock and his balls ached, but the discomfort was a small price to pay to see the immense pleasure on Alan's face. Craig was thrilled down to his soul to hear the happiness and contentment in Alan's voice when he stroked his fingers through Craig's hair and told him over and over how good he was and how proud of him he was.

In spite of the heavy ache between his legs and the need that still tried to claw its way out through his skin, or maybe because of it, Craig easily drifted off to sleep wrapped up in Alan's arms.

Craig walked into work the next morning with balls that still ached, an itch that needed to be scratched, but with strict instructions not to touch himself and none of that even began to sour his mood. In fact, it only made him smile bigger. Alan had been nothing but sweet to him that morning. Even though he'd issued the strict, *do not dare touch yourself, Little One*, order in his most delicious Daddy voice. He'd been the perfect boyfriend afterward. He made Craig breakfast and helped him shower and made sure he'd got to work on time.

Craig had barely swiped his card through the time clock before his uncle appeared out of nowhere. "Uncle Hank. You're back." Craig stepped into the open arms of his uncle and they hugged. "How are you? I wasn't expecting you until next week."

"Things wrapped up sooner than I expected, so I flew in last night." His Uncle furrowed his brow. "I called your cell, but you never answered."

Craig blushed. "I shut it off. Sorry. I was . . . ah . . . I was on a date." Craig wanted to shift the conversation in a different direction, but his Uncle had other ideas.

"A date? Well, you'll have to tell me all about it."

Craig winced when his uncle threw an arm over his shoulder. "My shift just started. I'm sure there's a guest somewhere who needs towels, or new soap or something. I have to get to work."

Hank tightened his grip when Craig tried to pull away. "There's a bunch of other people on shift who are fully qualified to deliver towels and kiss the ass of the rich. I'm taking you to the lounge for a coffee and you're going to tell me all about your date." Hank paused and cast him a wink. "Maybe not *all* about it. Spare me some details."

Craig laughed and threaded an arm around his uncle's waist and let himself be led to the lounge. It was good to have his uncle home, so good, that he found himself surprised to like the idea of introducing him and Alan.

"Hey, you did say to tell you *all* about it." Craig joked. His uncle was a great man and he had an open mind. But he supposed that even the most open minded individuals wouldn't want the details of their nephew's sex life. "It's good to have you back, Uncle Hank."

10
Alan

Steve stormed into Alan's office and dropped heavily into one of the chairs that sat across from his desk. Alan glanced at him, then glanced back at his computer. "Can I help you?"

"You had a date with the kid," when Alan cut him a sharp look Steve paused and corrected himself. "Okay, sorry. How did it go with Craig?" The corner of Alan's mouth twitched and Steve grinned. "You dirty dog. That pretty young thing really took a shine to you, huh?"

Alan leaned back in his chair. "He signed the contract." Alan debated telling Steve about their Daddy/boy relationship, but thought better of it. He wasn't sure how comfortable Craig would be with the idea of Alan sharing those personal details.

"No shit?"

"No shit."

Steve swept a hand over his bald head. "Damn, man. That's one hot sub you got there. Please tell me you tied him up and made him beg, or whipped him or flogged him or who the fuck am I kidding, that's not even your style. Man, you're lucky. You own this place. You can have your pick of any sub in here."

Alan's smile faltered. "Well, that's the thing. I think I'm going to sell the club."

Alan couldn't have surprised Steve more if he told him he was secretly in love with Steve's sister.

"Say again?"

"I'm selling the club." There. That sounded final. It was final. Alan realized last night, with Craig curled against him, happily sleeping, that he didn't want the club. Craig was right, he had no real reason to keep it and he'd only done so because he thought he should. Hell, that's why he bought it and he was tired of doing things because he thought he ought to do them. He wanted to *want* to do something.

"What the hell, Alan? Your club is your life."

Alan shook his head. "It was in the beginning. I must admit, I loved turning the place around and making it great again. That first month that we turned a profit, that was the best feeling of my life. But I never really wanted the club in the first place. It wasn't what I wanted then and it's not really what I want now."

Steve exhaled and leaned back in his chair. He looked like he'd aged ten years in the past two minutes. "What do you plan to do instead?"

Alan could only shrug. "I don't know, but I'm okay with not knowing."

Alan was surprised to see a slow, sly, smile spread across Steve's face. He leaned forward in the chair and rested his elbows on his knees. "Sell the club to me."

Alan's eyebrows shot up. "You?"

Steve nodded. "Me. I've been after you for years to renovate the place and put in a kitchen. Think of how long you could get people to stay if they didn't have to leave to eat. It would be a huge boost."

Alan raked his hand through his hair. "I know, but I didn't ever really have the desire to run a restaurant." Before Steve could interject he shot him a pointed look. "And you know you and I would never work well together. We're great friends and I'd like to keep it that way."

"So sell me the club. I'll do it myself."

"And that wouldn't be too taxing, having to run the restaurant down the street and this place?"

Steve shrugged. "I can roll both business into one brand. Sell the same food here that I do there. I always said The Dragon's Den was a good name for a kink club, so when I buy, I'll rebrand. I can bring staff here that's already trained from the restaurant. It'll be seamless. You have the second floor you never use, I can renovate that into the private playrooms, and the ones on the main floor can be converted to a kitchen. If I do the upstairs reno first, business can continue to chug along as usual and no profits will be lost during the renovations."

Alan took a deep breath. "You're sure about this?"

"Hell yeah, I'm sure. I'd be stupid not to do this. When you bought this place, it was a shit hole money pit and you turned it around. I know you had fun with it, but let's face it, Alan,

I'm not shocked that you're selling it, not after thinking about it. You're bored here. The challenge is gone. I remember the passion you had during those first years as you struggled to turn it around, and then when it started to succeed you were over the moon. But now it's doing well on its own and you're bored."

God yes. Alan thought. Steve was right. He was bored. The thrill was gone. When he'd first bought the club, it had been in dire straights, but Mike convinced him that they could turn it around. Mike, as it turned out, wasn't as enthusiastic about the actual business end of the business and wanted it more for a private playground, but Alan had thrown himself into it. The thrill of watching it evolve and improve and attracting new members had kept him going for years.

Alan grinned. "Have your lawyers call my lawyers and we'll get this going."

Steve seemed shocked. "Just like that?"

Alan nodded as he got to his feet. "I told you, Steve, I'm done doing things that don't make me happy, and that includes owning this place." He walked around his desk and pulled Steve up into a hug.

Steve was stiff at first, then laughed and threw his arms around Alan. "You're a crazy motherfucker you know that right. You take one look at this kid and suddenly you're handing him a contract and selling your business."

Alan stiffened in Steve's embrace and he must have felt it because he suddenly gripped Alan by the biceps and held him at arms length. "Listen to me, Alan. We have been friends a long damned time and I know you're probably expecting me to try and talk you out of this, or maybe you're waiting for me to list all the reasons why this is a bad idea, but fuck, Alan, I say go for it."

Alan wondered if he had been waiting for Steve to resist his decisions, or at least offer an argument against any of it, because when Steve didn't, Alan felt relieved. Steve grinned and tugged Alan into another hug.

"I want you to be happy."

Alan pulled out of the hug and grinned at Steve. "I think I am." His brow furrowed. "Is that stupid? I..."

Steve stuck his hand out and covered Alan's mouth. "No. You're not going to stand here and verbal-diarrhea all your doubts and shit so I can pat your back and dry your tears and tell you that you're wrong, because we both know you're being a fucking moron. You like the kid. So what if you haven't know him very long. I haven't seen you this happy in a long time."

Alan pulled Steve's hand off his mouth and watched as Steve wiped it on his pants. "Let me guess. Not since Mike."

Steve looked up at Alan and raised an eyebrow. "Nope. You were never this happy with Mike. Mike exhausted you. He pushed you about everything and I know I saw the kid for all of five seconds, but I don't think he'd ever push you. Encourage yes, browbeat... not a chance."

Alan leaned against the edge of his desk. "You think Mike pushed me?"

Steve rolled his eyes. "Please, Alan, use your brain. The club was his idea. The big fancy house you had to buy his half of was his idea. You giving him a stack of cash for the club and the house when you split was his idea. And that's just the tip of the iceberg. He was the brattiest fucking sub I'd ever seen and for the life of me I never could figure out how the two of you ended up together. You don't like the brats, they wear on your patience, and now it's worse now because they all remind you of Mike." Steve put a hand on Alan's shoulder and gave it a squeeze. "Have your lawyers call my lawyers and they can get the ball rolling. In the meantime, go find that sweet new toy of yours and play with him for a while."

Steve shot Alan another smile and walked out of his office and Alan dropped into his chair and closed his eyes. For a minute he wondered if he was having some sort of strangely early midlife crisis. First, he meets a sweet young man who he takes on as his boyfriend and his sub. Next, he agreed to sell his business to his best friend. The craziest thing of all, Alan realized as he scrubbed his face with his hands, was that none of it felt all that insane.

Anyone on the outside looking in might think that he'd lost his mind, but for the first time in a long time, Alan wanted something. He wanted Craig, and not for a little while. He wanted a life with him. The boy was already under his skin and etched into his bones and he'd sooner cut off one of his own limbs than let the man slip through his fingers.

Alan left work early and went home. He'd wished that he'd tried to convince Craig to come back to his place after work. At least then he'd have something to do. He could cook dinner for them both, instead of making a bowl of soup and a grilled cheese sandwich for himself. They could've spent the evening curled up under a blanket watching a movie, or maybe they'd go for a walk, or take a bath together. He knew it was probably stupid to miss someone so much who he barely even knew, but he did, and he missed getting to know him.

It was too early for dinner yet, so Alan settled down in front of the TV, not that there was anything good on. Alan had just finished flicking through the channels a second time when his phone vibrated on the coffee table. Alan glanced at the name on the screen, then at the clock. Craig wasn't due to be off work for another two hours, yet he'd just texted him. Alan grinned as he read the text.

Can I come by after work?

Alan took a breath and tried to steady his trembling hands so he could respond.

Of course. I'll cook us dinner. Sound good? Alan sent the text as he headed for the kitchen. He wanted to make something nice for Craig, something simple, but delicious. Alan was taking stock of the pantry when Craig's response came.

Sounds fantastic. See you soon.

Alan rummaged in the fridge and gathered the ingredients to make his favorite homemade baked macaroni and cheese. With two hours until Craig was off work, he had plenty of time to get it assembled and into the oven.

He flicked the radio on and got to work chopping the bacon. He was dumping the pasta in the boiling water before he realized that he had been grinning, and dancing, and completely enjoying himself in a way that he hadn't in a long time.

The idea of making a nice dinner for Craig had instantly thrilled him. He wanted to please Craig, to look after him if he had a bad day or to enjoy his company if he had a good day. He wanted to be a good Daddy for his boy.

Alan grinned at that thought. His boy. When he'd first thought of offering Craig a contract, never did he imagine that Craig would want that. It made sense though. He wasn't into the hardcore stuff. He wanted someone to be in charge and to look after him and Alan wanted someone to take care of, someone he could really connect with. Alan smiled. He felt like he'd found that with Craig. A balance of real life and the lifestyle with someone who would let him be as clingy and doting as he wanted to be.

Alan had the timing down to a science. By the time the cheese sauce was ready, the noodles could be drained, the two were mixed, smothered in yet more cheese and he stuffed it in the oven on a low temperature. He'd turn it up a little before Craig got there to make sure the cheese thoroughly melted.

When his doorbell rang shortly after six, Alan had just climbed out of the shower. He tugged his pants on and slid into his shirt before he answered the door.

Craig stood on the doorstep, his hands stuffed deep into his jacket pockets. "Hey."

"Hey you, come in." Alan stepped to the side and Craig hurried past him. "I thought you were off at six?"

"I was. I keep a change of clothes at work so I came straight over." He shrugged out of his jacket and Alan saw the uncertainty in his eyes. "I hope that's okay."

"It's more than okay." Alan took his coat and hung it in the closet. “Do you want something to drink? I can make you a tea or a coffee before I throw the salad together.”

“Tea thanks. I’ve had my fill of coffee for the day.”

Craig slid into his stool—in Alan’s mind that was his spot now and it would always be his spot. Alan got the tea going and started preparing the salad. Craig was quiet and seemed slightly preoccupied.

“How was work?”

Craig huffed a sigh and rolled his eyes. “Uncle Hank showed up today. He said his meetings wrapped up early, but he only said that because he thinks I’m too dumb to figure it out.”

Alan caught his eye and raised an eyebrow.

“He came back early to check on me, which is stupid, he could’ve called. Security told him about the Tim incident and he wanted to touch base with me.”

Alan focused on chopping the cucumber. “That doesn’t sound so terrible, so what are you really upset about?”

There was a long silence, Alan had quickly grown accustomed to that, to Craig needing time to gather his thoughts. Alan felt no need to hurry the conversation along, he could talk, or not talk to Craig all night long. All that mattered was that Craig was here and Alan got to look after him.

“He wants to meet you.”

“That doesn’t sound so terrible.” Alan said in what he hoped was his most reassuring voice. “You even offered to introduce us, eventually, just the other day. What changed to make you nervous?”

“He met Tim and he hated Tim. I don’t want him to hate you.”

Alan frowned and placed his hands on the counter. "Will his opinion of me affect yours?"

Craig shook his head. "Of course not."

Alan shrugged a shoulder. This was the first time felt the difference in their ages. He wanted to be patient with Craig's uncertainty, but it had been so many years since he'd sought out anyone's approval that he found Craig's desperation hard to relate to. "Then I don't give a shit. Let him hate me."

"Tim hated that Uncle Hank hated him. Of course, my uncle never came out and said as much to him, but Tim could tell, you know. I just..." Craig took a deep breath and finally forced himself to look at Alan instead of his own fidgeting fingers. "I want this to be different. I want everything about us to be nothing like it was with Tim and part of that is that Uncle Hank has to like you."

Alan felt for him, he really did. It had to be hell to be so totally devastated by a relationship that it left you quivering and questioning everything about the next one. "I could tell you that I'm not Tim until I'm blue in the face, but you're not going to listen to that." Alan gave the salad a quick toss and delivered it to the dining room table. He didn't want to be angry with Craig, but unless he understood, and fast, that he wasn't Tim and certainly wasn't going to do the things to Craig that Tim had done, Alan felt little hope that they could make this work in the long run. Alan needed to show Craig that he was different.

"I'll get the table set if you'd like a minute to wash up." Alan breezed past Craig who slowly climbed off the stool and disappeared down the hallway. Alan took a deep breath and set the table while Craig washed up. He was putting the dish of baked macaroni on the dining room table when Craig appeared in the doorway.

Alan turned around and Craig's head was lowered, his hands were stuffed in his pockets, Alan guessed it was to keep himself from fidgeting. "Dinner's ready. Come eat." Alan extended his hand to Craig, but he didn't take it. Instead he raised his head and looked at Alan with glassy eyes.

"You're mad at me, aren't you?"

And the bottom dropped out of Alan's heart. What was he going to do with this man? This poor, sweet man whose only crime had been loving the wrong man. Loving Tim had devastated Craig. It left him shaken to the core, even now. Though he was determined to move on, he couldn't shake the demons that Tim left behind. Alan strode over to Craig and gathered him in his arms and cradled him against his chest.

"I'm not mad at you, love, never, not for having feelings. You're allowed to feel however you need too and I'll never be angry with you for it."

11
Craig

CRAIG HATED FEELING LIKE this, like he wasn't enough. Wasn't good enough. Wasn't brave enough. Wasn't over Tim enough. Maybe he was over Tim, but there were things related to Tim that he hadn't gotten over.

But Alan tugged him close and Craig rested his head on Alan's chest and breathed him in and maybe, just maybe, he would be enough for Alan. He'd let all his quivering insecurities hang out and instead of scoffing at him or making him feel like less, Alan tugged him close and held him and told him he had the right to feel whatever emotions he was feeling. In that moment Craig believed that this could be different—was different—more different and more real than anything he'd ever felt.

He closed his eyes and took a deep breath, then one more because Alan smelled so fucking good, so fresh and clean that Craig wanted to climb into his lap and hold him and kiss him and do things to him that make them both messy and dishevelled. Instead, he looked up at Alan and smiled. "Next time I get stuck in my head I'm going to demand that you hug me." Craig slid his arms around Alan and raised himself up on his tiptoes. Alan met him halfway and they stood in the dining room, kissing until the food was cool enough to eat.

Craig loved kissing Alan. He loved that Alan was taller than him and he loved the way Alan held him tight with his large, powerful hands. He loved it when Alan's cheeks were smooth and freshly shaved and he loved kissing him when they had stubble that scratched at his skin. He loved the softness of his mouth and the way the intensity lit up every synapse in Craig's brain. In the past, kissing had been a means to an end, but kissing Alan could easily be a main event.

When the kiss came to an end Alan's arms were still wrapped around him and Craig sighed happily.

"Better?" Alan asked before planting a gentle kiss on Craig's forehead.

"Yeah. I am." The amount of conviction that came out in Craig's voice shocked himself a little. He was feeling better. Alan was so calm about everything and so matter of fact that it made it easy for Craig to believe him. Everything would be okay no matter what his uncle thought of Alan. "I'm starving."

Craig and Alan sat down to eat and for a few minutes Craig stayed quiet and let himself soak in the experience of eating with someone at a table like an adult. With Tim, they often ate in front of the television, or standing in the kitchen. Tim never took him out to eat and he certainly didn't cook for him. Then, when it was just him, he'd often grab a bite in the restaurant at the hotel, standing up in the corner or he'd take it to the break room and eat on one of the sofas. It didn't make sense, but it made him feel like him and Alan were as serious as they claimed to be.

"How was work?" Craig asked.

Alan shrugged a shoulder. "I'm selling the club to Steve."

He was completely nonchalant, as if he'd said that he got his car washed or took the trash out.

"Really? Isn't that a bit...sudden?" Craig stared at Alan and he seemed completely calm about it, as if it were any other decision like choosing a new fabric softener instead of a new career.

Alan took a drink of water and his eyebrow raised slightly. "Not really, I guess. I knew I was tired of the club, the challenge of turning it around was thrilling and exciting and I genuinely loved it, but it's time to move on. Steve wants to renovate the unused space upstairs and build a kitchen downstairs. He's convinced having a restaurant attached will be a huge draw and he's probably right. He's brought it up before, but kitchens and restaurants aren't my thing."

"If that's what you want, then I'm happy for you. Any ideas on what you're going to do once the sale is final?"

Alan shook his head. "Not really, but I have money saved. I won't need to worry about finding something different right away."

Craig wanted to be more enthusiastic for Alan. He wasn't happy at the club anymore and finding a new and exciting career was clearly important to him. The problem was that Craig didn't know what kind of career Alan would want. What if he wanted to do something that would take him away from here? What if he had to travel? Craig hated the idea of staying behind while Alan went away on business.

Craig shoved the thoughts aside. When he was a boy his mother had warned him about his tendency to borrow trouble, but he couldn't help it. His mind would get going and his imagination would take over his common sense and he'd often worry himself sick about things that might never happen.

"This is really good."

Alan reached over and put his hand on Craig's thigh. "What's wrong?"

Craig both loved and hated that Alan could read him so well. It gave him a sense of peace and comfort to know that he couldn't hide his moods from Alan. "I'm okay, it's been a really long and sort of strange week, that's all."

Alan's hand stroked Craig's thigh. "I know." His hand slid a little closer to Craig's cock. Craig tightened his grip on his fork and struggled to stay still. He really wanted to shift a little so that Alan's fingers would graze his erection. Any contact was better than the way he almost touched him where he needed it.

"It's been a good week, though, right, Little One?" Alan's voice sounded thicker and lower, as if lust and anticipation were already strangling him.

Little One. Not boy. Not something generic. Anyone could be boy, but only he could be little one. Oh god, yes. Craig latched onto the word that claimed him as Alan's and he let out a shaky breath. "It's been a very good week, Daddy."

"But you're stressed."

It wasn't a question, but Craig felt it required a response, so he nodded his head. "Yes, Daddy."

Alan's hand slid off his thigh and Craig immediately missed the heat from his palm.

"Eat your dinner." Alan's command was soft, but stern.

"Yes, Daddy." Craig's appetite vanished, but he ate dutifully anyway. Every so often, Alan would reach over and card his fingers through Craig's hair, or rub his thigh. Each time Craig's cock would get harder and thicker and it would get more and more difficult to eat.

By the time Craig finished eating, his cock was swollen and uncomfortable in the tight confines of his pants. Alan stood up from the table and gathered their empty plates. He paused and kissed Craig on the forehead. "Head upstairs, Sweetheart. I'll be along in a minute."

Craig stood, but paused, a flicker of uncertainty coursed through him. If they were going to do this, he didn't want to do it in the spare room, the pseudo-playroom, or whatever it had been to Alan and Mike. He wanted to be Alan's in every way and if they were going to do this he wanted to do it in Alan's room.

"Daddy?"

"What is it, Sweetheart?" Alan's forehead creased. Craig could tell that he was picking up on his nerves. He took a breath and did his best to steady himself.

"Do you think, I mean, can we . . . in your room, Daddy? I don't want to use the spare room." Craig looked at the floor, then, when he didn't immediately sink into it and vanish, he closed his eyes.

He heard Alan set the plates down, then approach him. Soft fingers traced the line of his jaw and Craig submitted to the gentle touch that tilted his head up. "Look at me."

Craig obeyed the smooth baritone. He couldn't help it if he tried. There was something about the sound of Alan's voice that reached into him and soothed him.

"You don't want to use the spare room?"

Craig did his best not to tremble. "No, Daddy."

"Why not? You were fine with it before. What changed?"

Craig swallowed and wished he could close his eyes and shrink away, or close his eyes and press himself closer to Alan. He wanted to be in his arms where he felt safe. "That was before I was yours."

Alan cupped Craig's chin, then leaned in and pressed a chaste kiss to his lips. "Then go on upstairs and strip down and wait for me in my room."

Craig did his best not to run up the stairs like an excited child. He wanted to show Alan that he could be mature and composed, but he couldn't help taking the stairs two at a time and he almost ripped his shirt he tore it off so fast.

He folded his clothes neatly and knelt on the floor. He did his best to remember how exactly he was supposed to do this, it had been awhile since he'd knelt and presented himself properly and he was more than a little excited. His cock was certainly into the idea of having his first proper scene with Alan. What they'd done so far had been hot and while he was glad that Alan had been willing to take things slow, Craig wanted to prove to Alan that he could satisfy him. Craig knew that as a Dom and a club owner, Alan had a lot more experience, but according to Alan that didn't matter. He said that he liked his lack of experience. All Craig had to do was submit and to trust that his submission would make up for his inexperience.

He forced himself to close his eyes and regulate his breathing. He bowed his head and waited. And waited. Finally, the door opened, and Alan came into the room. He resisted the urge to raise his head to look at Alan.

Craig leaned into Alan's familiar touch as he cupped his cheek.

"Such a beautiful boy. So eager to please Daddy, aren't you?"

"Yes, Daddy." God yes. He wanted to please Alan more than anything. He wanted to please him so bad he thought he might quiver out of his skin in anticipation.

Alan circled him. He touched his head, stroked his fingers through his hair, ran his hand across Craig's shoulders, then down his spine, stopping just shy of his ass. Alan's lips grazed the shell of Craig's ear and he inhaled sharply. "What if I told you that you already please me, Little One?"

Fuck. His heart was a goner and he knew it right then. There wasn't anything he wouldn't do for Alan, no matter if he was in Daddy mode or if they were hanging out as boyfriends. He wanted to make Alan happy. He wanted it more than anything. But he hadn't done anything, not really. Fear gripped him, and he trembled involuntarily.

"Sweetheart?"

"I'd ask why, Daddy? I haven't... we haven't... we've barely..." Craig pressed squeezed his eyes shut and bit his lip. He felt like he was already failing at this. He couldn't even answer a simple question.

"Stand up, Sweetheart." Alan's voice was firm, but his tone was gentle, and Craig got to his feet. He was ungraceful and still shaking as he did so, but he managed.

The next thing he knew, Alan had pulled him close and ran a hand down his back as the other cradled his head against Alan's chest. "You are so eager to please me that you're tying yourself up in knots over the possibility of not pleasing me. I need you to relax, can you do that for me, Little One?"

At that moment Craig thought could let himself be tied up and flogged or chained to a cross and caned before he'd be able to relax. "I can try, Daddy." He exhaled and let himself enjoy the warmth of Alan's bare chest. "For you, I can try."

Alan's hands roamed lower and they gave Craig's ass a playful squeeze. "I'll be right back."

Alan stepped out the door, but only for a moment. He returned with one of the dining room chairs and set it down behind Craig. "Have a seat."

Without hesitation, Craig sat in the chair. He looked up at Alan and decided that he liked this view of him the most. He liked it when Alan loomed over him. He seemed so composed and so powerful. Craig shivered at the thought of Alan losing control. He wondered what Alan would be like if he let himself go. Craig's mouth watered, and his dick hardened even more at the thought of Alan wild and blissed out.

Alan circled Craig as if he were prey. He watched as Alan crossed the room and opened one of his drawers. He returned with a handful of ties and dropped them unceremoniously into Craig's lap. Wordlessly, Alan arranged Craig so that his ass was only half on the seat. He leaned him back, so his shoulders rested on the back of the chair. Craig shivered when Alan dragged his hands down Craig's legs and arranged them so his feet were next to the legs of the chair.

Craig's cock strained upward, and Craig's breathing became shallow as Alan knelt in front of him and carefully grabbed a tie off Craig's lap. Craig's eyes widened, and his pulse sped as Alan secured his ankles to the legs of the chair. Still kneeling, Alan looked at Craig and ran his hands along the outside of Craig's thighs. Alan leaned in and brushed a soft kiss against Craig's lips as he retrieved two more ties from his lap.

Craig shut his eyes when Alan stood and circled around behind him. Alan used the ties to secure Craig's arms to the back legs of the chair. Still behind him he leaned down and Craig shivered as his lips caressed the outer shell of his left ear.

"Comfortable, Little One?"

"Yes, Daddy."

Craig arched his back into Alan's gentle touch when his hands ran down Craig's chest. He tilted his head back and soaked in the euphoric feeling that filled him.

Alan retrieved the last tie from Craig's lap and the silky fabric tickled his skin as Alan dragged it up his torso. "I'm going to blindfold you again. I want you to sit there and relax and feel and listen to me. Can you do that?"

"Yes, Daddy."

The fabric was cool against his skin as Alan covered his eyes. "Tell me your safe word."

Craig swallowed a thick lump of nerves that took up residence in his throat. When he was with Tim he had to choose his own safe word, but he didn't want to use that here. Not with Alan.

"Can we use the stoplights, Daddy? They're easy to remember. Green is go. Yellow is slow down. Red is stop."

Alan chuckled softly. "That's fine, Sweetheart." Warm lips touched the top of Craig's bare shoulder. "I want you to close your eyes and relax."

Alan circled Craig, but his hands never left him. Alan's fingertips breezed across the tops of Craig's shoulders. Then Alan flattened his hands and raked them down Craig's chest. Alan's lips danced across his collarbone and goosebumps erupted when Alan's breath washed over his skin.

"Black looks amazing on your skin, too." Alan stroked his hand over the ties the bound his wrists, eliciting a shiver of pleasure from Craig. "You're so beautiful." Alan barely breathed the words, but they sank into Craig's heart and he clutched them tight. He *felt* beautiful. He almost wanted to cry because he'd never felt beautiful before. He'd never felt so appreciated just for existing until he met Alan. Alan never made him feel as if he were doing something wrong. He never felt as if he were falling short of Alan's expectations.

Alan's fingertips flicked over Craig's nipples. The sensation sent shock waves to his cock and his entire body twitched.

A rumble of pleasure rippled out of Alan and he repeated the motion. Craig inhaled sharply. "Fuuuuuck." Craig couldn't stop the word from sliding past his lips any more than he was able to contain the way his back arched into Alan's touch or the warmth that heated his chest. He let his head roll back and rest on the back of the chair.

"You're so perfect." Alan's hands explored lower. His fingers danced across Craig's abs. Craig chuffed a laugh when they danced across his belly button. He groaned when Alan's fingers travelled lower. They skimmed down the side of his stomach and into the crease of his thighs, then lower. Craig wanted Alan's hand wrapped around his cock. He wanted to feel those powerful hands on his aching cock, but Alan had other ideas.

Feather-light touches danced down the insides of his thighs. A huff of hot air washed over his balls. Craig whimpered and barely resisted the urge to thrust his hips. Then Craig did lose control and thrust into the air when Alan's hands skimmed up his thighs until they framed his cock. A delicate touch, fingers toyed with his thatch of dark hair.

"I'm going to shave this one day."

Craig's chest heaved as he groaned.

"Can you imagine how that would feel?"

Hot breath caressed Craig's cock. He was so close he almost felt the brush of Alan's lips on his skin.

"Can you imagine the way my hands would feel on you as I spread the shaving cream. Cold cream on hot skin." Alan made a sound that was almost a purr.

"Ung." Craig's attempt at a coherent word was thwarted when Alan leaned forward and flicked the underside of his cock with his tongue.

"God," Alan groaned. "The way you'd tremble as the razor would scrape against your skin. It would light you up from the inside out. You'd be so beautiful and sensitive after." Alan's hand wrapped around the base of Craig's cock.

"Oh God. Oh fuck." Craig's head lolled back and forth.

Alan's laughter was low and husky. He sounded as if

he were as affected as Craig was. Wound tight, his body thrummed with barely contained need.

Alan dragged his hand up Craig's cock as his tongue swirled around the head.

"All that hair stripped away. Your pretty cock all naked and hard for me."

Craig twitched so hard the chair creaked when Alan's fingers brushed against Craig's balls. The gentle touches combined with Alan's deep, soothing voice, laced with husky need drove Craig closer to the edge. They filled him and coursed through his veins like a drug. Maybe Alan was a drug. Since he'd walked into Craig's life everything was brighter, lighter, easier.

Alan continued to assault Craig's senses with his smooth husky voice and his expert touches. Fire built in Craig's stomach and slowly spread outward. Up his chest, down his trembling thighs, and up his rock-solid erection.

Craig's wrists tugged at the restraints and he struggled to keep his eyes closed when Alan's hot, wet, mouth encased Craig's cock and took it all in.

"Oh fuck." Craig panted and thrust his hips, but Alan quickly tossed an arm around his middle and pinned his restless hips down.

"Oh God. Oh shit. Your mouth. Oh fuck, Daddy, I'm . . ."

Every muscle in Craig's body stiffened and twitched. Then Alan's mouth came off Craig's cock with the lewd slurping sound of lips breaking suction. His touch simultaneously vanished. Craig's chest heaved. "Fuck." The word came out choked and Alan chuckled. He placed his hands on the tops of Craig's knees and slowly slid them up his thighs.

"Thought I told you to stay still." Alan said, and Craig stopped struggling. His breathing was still erratic, and he balled his hands into fists.

"Sorry. Fuck. Sorry, I was so close."

"Mmmmm," Alan moaned. "I'm not sure what's sexier. Watching every muscle in your body twitch, or that desperate edge your voice gets when you're so close to falling apart." Alan gripped Craig's cock again and gave it a languid pump.

Craig jerked in his restraints. "Fuck."

"You have a filthy mouth, Little One." Alan didn't sound upset. He continued with the slow and lazy way he tortured Craig's cock. Craig's body thrummed with need that only seemed to build the slower Alan stroked.

"Shit." Craig twitched when Alan's tongue slicked along his tight sack. "And you say I have a filthy mouth. Goddamn, that's gonna . . ." A desperate desire spread through him and felt like flames licked his entire body. Hot all over and right near the edge, he was so close to losing control, but like before, Alan sensed his impending orgasm, and all contact ceased.

"You should see yourself. All flushed and on edge. You're so wild right now, so desperate." Alan kissed the crease of Craig's thigh. His words were a balm on Craig's charred heart, but the tender kiss was what touched him the most. Alan had never been anything but gentle and generous with Craig, but that kiss felt like more. It was as if the kiss spoke all the things that Alan hadn't said, and it made Craig feel precious.

Alan's hands returned, and his ministrations continued, but Craig could tell by the movement that Alan's control might be slipping. Craig wanted it to slip. He wanted Alan to need him with the same ferocious need that coursed through his veins and strangled his words.

"Can I . . . can we . . . God, Daddy. I need you. Please."

The ties on his ankles were the first to vanish. Then Alan quickly released his wrists. Before he could get a word in, Alan pulled Craig off the chair and into his arms.

12
Alan

Some Dom Alan was. He was supposed to be in control. He'd intended to edge Craig until he was red, trembling, and desperate for release. Then, and only then, would he allow the boy to fly. But then he'd begged, and Alan couldn't hold out any longer. He needed him. He ached for Craig in a way that made it seem wrong to leave him bound and begging.

He kissed him with a ferociousness that surprised Craig. He took advantage of the sexy way Craig gasped and slid his tongue through his parted lips. Craig melted into him. The only thing keeping Craig upright was Alan. In his arms, Craig was pliant. Even his mouth submitted. Craig's tongue caressed Alan's as it explored.

Craig's arms wrapped around Alan's neck. Fingers slid up into his hair as Alan kissed his way down Craig's jaw. He flicked Craig's earlobe with his tongue and Craig's fingers tightened in Alan's hair. Craig moaned. The sound was full of desperation, desire, and pure need. It was music to Alan's ears. He scooped Craig up into his arms and carried him to the bed.

"I wanted to edge you into oblivion, but God, Little One, I can't." Alan said as he set Craig down on the bed. He quickly undid his pants and slid out of them, then yanked his shirt off. "I need you. I need to touch you and kiss you and possess you."

Still blindfolded, Craig scooted up the bed a little, then leaned back on his elbows. "I need you, too. So much, Daddy."

Daddy. Alan never for a moment considered how much it would turn him on to hear that word come out of Craig's needy mouth. He was beautiful with his lust-flushed cheeks and his kiss-swollen lips. And he was his. Alan's boy. His Little One. His Sweetheart.

Alan crawled up the bed and straddled Craig. He leaned in and pressed a kiss to the corner of his mouth. He didn't know what he did to deserve him, but he'd always be thankful for Craig and the way he'd crashed into his life.

"Lay back." Lay back and let me love you, Alan thought, but it was too early for such declarations. He could love Craig though. The thought should scare him, but it didn't. He wanted to love Craig. There was something about Craig that drew Alan to him, an invisible string connected them. He'd felt the pull the moment his eyes landed on Craig. All he wanted to do since he'd met him was wrap him up in his arms and never let him go. He wanted to possess Craig in ways that he'd never fathomed before.

Alan took his time exploring Craig's body. He loved his soft skin and his trim figure. Craig wasn't too thin, or too muscled. He was that perfect combination of hard muscle and soft angles.

Craig's hands twitched at his sides. "Daddy, please."

Alan cupped Craig's cheek. When Craig leaned into his touch, Alan's heart did a kick-flip. Socially acceptable time lines of how soon you could fall in love with someone could rot. Craig *was* his. He was so earnest in everything he said and did, and Alan loved him for it. "Yes, Baby. What do you need?"

Craig exhaled and if possible, relaxed even more. "I need to please you."

Alan stroked Craig's cheek. "You do please me."

Craig's twitching fingers reached for Alan. They tickled their way up Alan's side. "Let me please you. I want to."

Desperate to see all of Craig, Alan removed the blindfold. Craig blinked a couple times and Alan couldn't resist stealing a kiss. Alan cupped his cheek, his thumb stroked along Craig's cheekbone. Alan's heart flooded with warmth when Craig leaned into the touch.

"I want those beautiful lips around my cock."

Craig's eyes fluttered shut and he exhaled. "God, yes. Please."

Alan stroked his hand down the side of Craig's neck. He let his fingers trace the slant of his collarbone before they ventured lower. His hand came to a stop right above Craig's heart, the part of the man he really wanted to own. "Stay still."

Alan leaned down and stole a fleeting kiss then shimmied up the bed. He gripped the headboard with one hand as he straddled Craig's chest. He wrapped the fingers of his free hand around his cock. He didn't need to command Craig to open for him, his eyes were already glassy with lust and his lips were parted. Slowly, Alan lowered his cock to Craig's lips and slid the head across Craig's lower lip.

Craig's mouth opened farther, and Alan accepted the wordless invitation. He slid his cock into Craig's mouth, then let go of his cock to grip the headboard. "Fuck yes." Craig didn't move while Alan thrust his hips, gently stroking his cock in and out of Craig's mouth.

Craig remained motionless. Their gazes locked, and it was all Alan could do not to ram his cock deep into Craig's throat, but he didn't want to gag him. Craig was too beautiful like this. Though he rode lust's razor edge, he looked blissed out. Alan liked knowing that he didn't have to go hardcore Dom to get a reaction out of Craig.

"God, you're so fucking perfect." Alan groaned and thrust a little deeper. Craig winced, but didn't gag. "Suck me. Now."

Craig got a wicked look in his eyes. His lips closed around Alan's throbbing cock. His tongue swirled around the head, caressing every curve and igniting every nerve ending. Alan's body told him to close his eyes and throw his head back, but he fought. He kept his eyes open. He wanted to watch Craig. He wanted to memorize the way his eyes gleamed with pleasure when Alan hissed or the way he almost smiled when Alan moaned.

"Your mouth." Alan gripped the headboard until his knuckles turned white. "Fuck. Your mouth. So good."

Craig's hands slid up Alan's legs. He glanced at one, then looked back at Craig, who raised an eyebrow. Then Craig's hands gripped Alan's ass and Craig sucked Alan harder, deeper.

"Oh shit. Fuck." Alan bucked. Craig gagged, but recovered quickly. Alan's control was on the ragged edge. The way Craig's tongue caressed his cock, the way his hands felt as they kneaded his ass, his fingers igniting fires of lust as they grazed his crease, it was too much. It consumed Alan. He squeezed his eyes shut as ecstasy unfurled inside him. "Oh. Fuck. Baby. Oh shit." Alan barked as his orgasm slammed into him. His whole body shook and trembled as he came down Craig's throat. His head flopped forward, and he panted. Craig had totally wrecked him.

He opened his eyes and Craig stared up at him. Craig blinked, and a few tears slipped away from the corner of his eyes. "God, Sweetheart." He panted as he gently pulled out. "That was fucking amazing."

A smile spread across Craig's face. Alan thought Craig was beautiful to begin with, but like this, beneath him, smiling, red faced with his swollen lips, Craig lit Alan up. Craig was his and he wasn't ever going to let him go.

Craig licked his lips and tucked his hands behind his head. "You really think so, daddy?"

Alan couldn't help but smile. "Yes, I do. But now it's your turn."

Craig's cheeks pinked. "Actually, Daddy . . . um . . ."

Alan glanced down and sure enough, Craig's formerly jutting cock looked as sated as Alan's was, though it did give a valiant little kick when Alan looked at it. His stomach was coated in cum. Alan glanced back at Craig. "You came?" More realizations piled on and Alan moved so that he was laying next to Craig. "You came without touching yourself, and without permission." Alan raised an eyebrow and Craig immediately dropped his gaze. His face paled slightly.

"Sorry, Daddy."

Alan leaned over and kissed Craig on the cheek. "That's fucking hot." He laughed and pulled Craig closer to him. He tossed a leg over Craig's and an arm around his waist. "What's the matter?"

Craig was quiet for a while and Alan didn't pressure him. He let Craig gather his thoughts and catch his breath. Craig sighed. "I didn't want to disappoint you."

Alan pulled Craig closer and kissed the top of his head. "You couldn't possibly disappoint me."

Craig tensed. "I begged you. You wanted to edge me into oblivion and I begged for more. Then I came without permission."

Alan resisted the urge to squeeze Craig any tighter than he already was. "And I enjoyed every single moment with you, Little One." Alan took a deep breath. "We're connected, you and me. We're connected in ways that I've never felt before."

"But you're my Dom. My Daddy. There's like... rules and stuff... for me, for submissives, and I feel like I keep breaking them."

Alan carded his fingers through Craig's hair. "The last time I was in a scene with a submissive was more than half a year ago." Craig twitched in his arms, but stayed quiet, as if he sensed that this was a story Alan needed to tell. "I'd been in scenes with other subs since Mike and I broke up, but I was falling out of love with the whole thing, to be honest. I didn't realize it until I had him, the submissive I was with, strapped to a cross. He was naked and waiting for me to pick up my flogger and work him over. But I couldn't. I couldn't even pick it up. I stood there, and I realized that I felt nothing.

Absolutely nothing. I was totally empty. I let the submissive down from the cross and went home and I haven't even so much as glanced at a sub since. Until you."

Craig pulled away a little and looked at Alan. His brown eyes were round and large and full of hope. "Me?"

"When you walked into my club and you knelt that first time, God, Sweetheart, it was like you turned all my lights back on. I've been a Dom for a lot of years, and yeah, it's amazing to have you kneel at my feet and call me Daddy. It's thrilling to command you and your submission is the most beautiful thing in the world. But you, Craig, *you* are what I want. *You* are what am connected to, not your submission, not the rules we create in our relationship. You. You're what's important to me. Besides, you wanted to take things slow and I'm okay with that. I'm okay with going slow and earning your trust."

Craig looked at him with shining eyes and a tear tracked down his cheek. "I do trust you."

"Then trust me when I say this. You are enough. You're absolutely everything I need, and I don't want you to ever doubt that, okay?"

Craig wiggled around and buried his face against Alan's chest. He took a deep breath. "Okay."

* * *

"Are you sure I look okay?" Alan smoothed his black polo shirt down. "You said not to dress up, but I can't imagine meeting your uncle in jeans and a T-shirt."

Craig shook his head as he laughed. "Relax. You look fine." Craig eyed Alan appreciatively.

"But you want him to like me. It's important to you that he does, so it's important to me, too."

Craig entwined their fingers and led Alan toward the dining room. "I do want him to like you, but I realized something recently."

"What's that?"

Craig turned and pressed a kiss to Alan's lips in front of the whole dining room. "I don't give a shit. I like you and that's all that really matters."

"Oh, you like me, do you?" Alan wrapped an arm around Craig's wait and hauled him close.

"Maybe a little."

Craig practically sparkled today, and Alan couldn't get over the change in him. From the moment Alan met him, he knew that Craig wore his heart on his sleeve. It was never hard to guess exactly how he was feeling. When he met Craig, he could see that the way he'd been hurt weighed him down. Alan saw it in his eyes and heard it in his voice and even noticed it in the way he moved. This morning Craig woke him up with a blow job. He washed Alan in the shower and sang the whole time. When they made breakfast this morning, Craig turned on music and shook his tight ass all over Alan's kitchen.

Alan broke away from his thoughts to capture Craig in a kiss. "You are absolutely wonderful did you know that?"

"I've been telling him that for years, but if you saying it puts that dopey look on his face, then I like you already." Craig's eyes widened at the sound of the voice. Alan turned around and greeted the smiling man. He was clearly related to Craig, and if Alan hadn't have known better, he'd have guessed that this was Craig's father, not his uncle. "I'm Hank, and you must be Alan. Craig's told me a lot about you." Hank winked at Craig. "Not willingly, mind you. I had to drag it out of him."

Hank was a little taller than Craig, and a little thicker in the middle, greyer on top, but there was a strong family resemblance. They had the same cheekbones and the same eyes. "It's good to meet you, Hank." Alan shook his hand, then watched as Hank pulled Craig into a quick hug.

Hank pulled away and clapped Craig on the arm. "Let's eat."

They followed Hank to a table on the fringe of the dining room where they were immediately greeted by a server. Conversation stuck to small talk until the coffee they'd ordered had arrived. Hank spooned some sugar into his cup, then lifted his gaze and trained it on Alan. "So, what have you done to my boy here?"

Alan raised an eyebrow. "I beg your pardon?" Alan knew this conversation could go many ways and he doubted that many of them were good. Then Hank grinned over top of his cup.

"I only asked because Craig is actually smiling. And this is the first time in months that I haven't had to chase him out of here on his day off."

"I'm not that bad." Craig's protest was weak, and Hank immediately quashed it.

"Not that bad? Please, Craig. I might not be here all the time, but I hear things. You've been a pain in the ass around here. You work yourself sick. You don't delegate anything unless you absolutely must, and I don't know how many times I've heard that they've had to toss you out on your day off."

Craig's cheeks flushed, and he stared into his coffee. "I guess I was sort of bad, huh?"

Hank reached over and patted Craig on the back. "Worse." Hank shot Alan a knowing glance. "It looks like you've found yourself a nice distraction. Tell me about yourself, Alan. What do you do?"

"Well, I run a club down town, but I'm actually in the process of selling it. After that," Alan shrugged. "I don't actually know." Alan's cheeks burned with a hint of embarrassment, but he'd never hid what he did for a living and he wasn't about to start now.

Hank regarded him with curiosity. "Why are you selling?

"In the beginning, it was a lot of fun, actually. The club was run down and failing. Every month ended in the red. It took a while to turn it around completely, but the challenge of making it successful was, frankly, exhilarating." Alan took a sip of his coffee. "I'm selling it to a friend of mine. He has big plans for it."

"So you took a dying business, turned it around, and are selling it for a tidy little profit and you have no idea what you're doing next?" Hank leaned back in his chair. He tilted his head slightly, as if he were a curious dog.

Alan shrugged a shoulder. "The club will sell for a profit, and I have some money saved. I don't need to decide right away."

Hank leaned forward. "But if an opportunity presented itself, you'd consider it?"

Alan raised an eyebrow. Hank was on a fishing expedition and Alan took the bait. “What kind of opportunity?”

“I have the opportunity to invest in a failing chain of smaller hotels. I toyed with the idea of buying them out and rolling them into this chain, but I have too much on my plate. I’d need someone who was up to the task. Someone who was familiar in bailing out failing companies. Someone who was up to the challenge.”

Alan’s heart sped up, but he forced himself to remain sceptical. If it sounded too good to be true, it often was. “That sounds like an ambitious endeavour.”

Hank nodded. “It would be, and I think you’re the right man for the job.”

Alan eyebrows scrunched together.

“Uncle Hank, are you seriously offering my boyfriend a job?” Craig looked incredulous.

Alan reached under the table and put his hand on Craig’s thigh. Craig put his hand on top of Alan’s. “How do you know I’m the man for the job? We’ve spent all of five minutes together.”

Hank grinned slyly at Alan, then took a sip of his coffee. “I have friends who frequent your establishment. I’ve heard stories about the place. From what I hear you’ve achieved the impossible. It used to be a cesspool and a money pit, but you managed to pull it out of the gutter. I’m impressed.”

Alan hadn’t been expecting that. Clearly, neither had Craig, who closed his mouth so hard his teeth clacked together.

Hank shrugged a shoulder. “We can talk about all that later.” Hank’s eyes skirted from Alan to Craig. “You look well, better than you have in a long time.”

Alan watched Craig bristle slightly at his uncle's words, but then Craig shot Alan a look from the corner of his eye before he grinned at his Uncle. "I'm actually pretty great, but you didn't force me to bring Alan here, so you could fawn all over me."

Hank set his cup down. "Actually, Craig, I did. I know I probably came on a little strong yesterday, but you know me. When I get hot under the collar like that, there's no reasoning with me. I was upset that you had a problem here at work with that slimy son-of-a-bitch you call an ex-boyfriend. No matter my feelings about Tim, you're an adult. I didn't have a right to show up out of the blue, pull you off the floor and interrogate you like a child. You handled the situation perfectly, and I knew that when security made me aware of the incident. I'm not sorry I checked on you though. I can see now that you're a lot happier," Hank winked at Craig. "I'm not sorry to see you happy."

The food arrived, breaking up the conversation. Alan eyed Hank. From what Craig said, Hank could be a tough nut to crack, but he'd yet to show any animosity toward Alan, and had even offered him a job . . . potentially. Alan still hadn't come to terms with that tid-bit of information.

The rest of lunch seemed to flow a bit smoother now that the topics of work and Craig's shitty ex had been dropped. Alan found that he like Craig's uncle. He was quick witted and had a million stories to tell about his various adventures around the country. What Alan enjoyed the most was watching Craig hang off his uncle's every word.

Alan pushed his empty plate away and looked at Craig. "Did you ever want to travel?"

Craig shrugged a shoulder. "I've entertained the idea."

"Why don't you?" asked Alan. From the corner of his eye he watched Hank, who had his full attention trained onto Craig.

Craig poked at the last of his food with his fork. "To me, travel would be great, but I'd like to stay places long enough to actually experience them." Craig shrugged again and loaded his fork. "I wouldn't want to go alone either. Travelling, to me, it seems like something I'd want to share with someone." Craig shoved the fork in his mouth as Hank's phone rang.

Hank answered his phone and informed whoever was on the other end that he'd call them back in ten minutes. He rose from the table. "I hate to run out on the two of you, but I really do have to return that call." He shook Alan's hand then yanked Craig into a hug and clapped him on the back. "I have to leave town week after next, get in touch with me before then." Hank glanced at Alan before letting go of Craig. "You too. I'd like to discuss that ambitious endeavour of mine in more detail."

Hank walked away as he dialled his phone.

Alan sighed with relief. He turned to Craig and offered a weak smile. "So. I don't think he hates me." Alan expected Craig to show some relief, but he seemed to be stressed more now than he had been earlier. He grabbed Craig's hand and threaded their fingers together. "I have to go see my lawyer in a bit and get the paperwork going for the sale of the club. We can meet for dinner if you'd like."

Craig squeezed his hand. "I haven't really seen Everett in a while. I should check on him."

"Everett?"

Craig laughed. He sounded awkward and a little nervous. "He's my neighbor. He's the one who let me know Tim had stopped by. We met when I moved into the building. We hang out a lot, but I haven't really been around recently." Craig glanced at Alan.

"Ah. Point taken. You feel like you've been ditching your friend?"

"A little." Craig's shoulders slumped a little when he sighed.

When the exited the hotel, Alan pulled Craig off to the side and yanked him into his arms. "Go see your friend." He kissed the shell of Craig's ear and relished the little shiver that rocketed through Craig. "I'll call you later tonight, okay."

Craig rested his forehead against Alan's chest and he felt him nod. "Okay. Sounds good. Tell me how it goes with the lawyers, okay?"

"Promise. Do you want a lift home? I have time to take you before I meet the lawyer."

Craig pulled away and kissed him quickly. "It's okay. I have to run a couple of errands."

Alan reluctantly let Craig go. Parting with the words *I love you, see you later,* would've been nice, but he had to bite them back. They weren't at that point in their relationship yet. As Alan turned and walked away from Craig he couldn't fight the ball of regret that built in the pit of his stomach. He should've told him. He shouldn't care so much that he fell so fast, but if he was honest with himself he would be able to admit the truth. He didn't say the words because he was afraid that Craig wouldn't say them back.

13

Craig

CRAIG'S ERRAND WAS A trip to the liquor store for a bottle of wine for him and Everett to share. Craig couldn't get the image of Alan walking away out of his head. It was stupid. He knew it was. He recognized how irrational he was being. Alan wasn't Tim. Alan wasn't about to drop him like a hot potato and jet off to do the job his uncle offered him.

Craig gripped the bottle tighter as he thumped up the stairs to his apartment. What was his uncle doing anyway, offering Alan a job as he did? The job would take Alan away from Craig. Was that his uncle's plan? Did he not approve of Alan? Was the job a way to get rid of him? Craig shook his head. Nothing made sense anymore, which was why he needed to see Everett. In the months that they'd known each other, Everett had frequently been the shoulder that Craig cried on.

He knocked on Everett's door and waited. His friend answered a minute later wearing only an apron. The sight might have been unusual to anyone else, but Craig was used to Everett answering the door like this. He was *The Crock Cock*, the internet's hottest, gayest, and most naked chef. His vlog had a hundred thousand subscribers and Everett was able to live solely off the income it brought in. There was even a whisper lately of sponsorships and television deals, but Everett wasn't counting his chickens before they hatched.

Everett cocked an eyebrow when he noticed the wine. He stepped aside and motioned for Craig to come in. "Good timing. I'm wrapping up my shoot. Make yourself comfy, uncork that bad boy, and I'll be with you in three minutes."

Craig toed his shoes off and pushed them off to the side. Everett placed a couple of wine glasses and a corkscrew on the coffee table then hurried back to the kitchen. Craig worked on uncorking the wine while his friend filmed the out-tro of his video.

It was no wonder why Everett had a huge following. He had a clean cut, charming, boy next door sort of vibe going on, but his smile was always wolfish and paired well with his innuendo laden cooking vlogs.

By the time Craig got the wine uncorked and filled the two glasses Everett had finished filming. He slipped into his room and returned a moment later in a pair of sweats that hung low on his hips and a faded Superman T-shirt that had seen better days. Black bondage cuffs hugged Everett's wrists. The only time Everett took them off was when he filmed for his cooking vlog.

Everett took his glass of wine, curled up in his recliner with his legs tucked underneath himself. His immediately drank half of his wine. "Are you going to tell me where you've been running off too lately?"

Craig's cheeks flushed. He hid his grin behind his glass. "Remember when I stayed out all night not too long ago? I met someone."

Everett's eyebrows raised in surprise, then the corner of his mouth tilted in amusement. "Good for you, man. Tell me about him. Does he tie you up and whip you? Or is he one of those guys that prefer you on all fours with a cute little puppy tail wagging away as he makes you crawl around?"

Craig shook his head. Sometimes he wondered if telling Everett about his kinkier side had been the right decision. "You're impossible, you know that, right?"

Everett leaned back. He used his free hand to shove his hair off his forehead. "Seriously, Craig. Tell me about him. You know I'm the last person who is going to judge you, right?"

Craig knew Everett was in the lifestyle, though he never shared any specifics and Craig never pushed. All he knew was that Everett was far kinkier than Craig ever thought of being and that he didn't do clubs. Which meant he had other ways of meeting Doms, probably those freaky apps that scared the shit out of Craig.

Craig sighed. "I feel like a shit. I can't seem to stop comparing him to Tim. I do it all the time and I tell myself to stop, but everything he does is so different, so much better that I can't help it."

Everett took a sip of his wine. "It's natural to compare one relationship against another. Especially when it's new and you're still figuring things out. It doesn't help that things with Tim ended so abruptly and with so little closure for you."

"Alan is nothing like him. He's not hardcore the way Tim was. He doesn't want to Dom all the time. He used to, but I think both of our past relationships changed what we want going forward." Craig refilled his empty wine glass. If he were seriously going to sit there and talk about his sex life he needed alcoholic fortification. "Neither one of us want hardcore, full-time, BDSM." Craig confessed.

"You say you both want the same thing, so what's worrying you?"

Craig took a deep breath. "He owns a club, Ev. He's selling it, and my uncle offered him a job, but he's owned a club for years. He's got way more experience and I know he said he wants a real relationship with a dash of kink, but I can't help but worry that I'm not enough."

Everett whistled. "Shit, dude. That's a lot to unpack." He drained the rest of his wine and stretched out so Craig could refill it. "Obviously the guy is into you, he met your uncle."

"Good point."

"So why don't you think you're enough? Is it because he owns a club?"

Craig raked a hand through his hair. "He's been a Dom for years. He used to have a full-time submissive. You know my experience," Craig scoffed. "I barely have any and I'm super picky about my limits. I'm a terrible sub. I keep telling him this, but he says he doesn't mind. One day though, what if he does mind?" Craig knew the answer to that. One day, Alan was going to mind and then he'd leave. Like Tim had.

Everett frowned, but before he could comment, Craig went off on a tangent. He'd finished spilling his guts and needed to redirect the conversation for a minute. "He showed up at the hotel."

"Who?" Everett asked. "Tim?"

"Yeah. Not long after he was here he cornered me at work. He said we needed to talk, but I had him thrown out. I'm not interested in anything he has to say. Not after what he did."

Everett gracefully unfolded himself and got up off the recliner. He set his wine glass down on the coffee table and plopped down on the couch next to Craig. He slung a slender arm around Craig's shoulders and tugged him close. "I know you're freaked out. Tim really hurt you. Being broken up with is one thing, but the way Tim did it was especially cruel. But if you've been this unsure around Alan, then I bet that he's as confused as I am. You need to decide what you want and then go for it. Alan isn't a mind reader."

Craig set his glass on the table next to Everett's. His stomach churned and frothed like an ocean during a storm. "Uncle Hank offered him a job. A job that probably requires travel. Alan is selling the club. He'll probably take the job." Craig clasped his hands together. "Where does that leave me?"

"There's Skype. Besides, it doesn't sound like Alan is exactly hurting for cash. He'll probably be back to see you all the time. Or you could fly out and see him. But you really shouldn't borrow trouble, Craig. Nothing is decided yet. Alan might reject the offer, or it might not be what you think it is."

Craig sighed. He couldn't help but feel a little crestfallen. So many times in his life he felt as if he'd found everything he'd been looking for and each time it ended up slipping through his fingers. Tim had been the worst of it though. Even before Tim did leave Craig felt like he was losing Tim. It was a truth it took him a long time to accept. Craig closed his eyes and took a deep breath as Everett gripped his shoulder. The weight of his arm across his back gave him a little comfort.

"I don't want to lose him, Everett. Tim and I… we were doomed. We never were going to make it. He figured that out before I did, though. But Alan, I think we can. We really mesh, you know. We seem to want all the same things, but you're right. I'm scared."

"Then you'll have to find a way to trust him, Craig. That's all there is to it."

Craig snorted. "Yeah, because trust is so easy, right."

Everett shrugged a shoulder. "It's not called a leap of faith for nothing."

Both Craig and Everett turned their head when someone knocked on Everett's door.

Everett furrowed his brow. "I have no idea who that could be. You're basically the only person I know. Well, there's Andrew and Xavier, but Andrew left yesterday to help Xavier pack up his stuff."

"Andrew and Xavier?"

Everett hoisted himself off the couch and started toward the door. "Andrew is my childhood best friend and Xavier is his kid brother. He recently finished culinary school and he's moving in with Andrew."

The pounding on the door became more aggressive and Everett yelled out that he was coming. "Sheesh. No one has any patience these days."

Craig watched as Everett put his face to the door and looked out the peephole. Everett turned, his face a little whiter. The hairs on the back of Craig's neck stood up.

"It's Tim and he doesn't look so good."

Craig balled his fists and nodded his head. "Let him in."

Everett undid the security chain and opened the door and stepped aside. Craig watched as Tim swayed. He put one hand on the wall for support as Everett closed the door and locked it behind him.

"Everett. I think you should call the police." Craig said as he wrapped his arms around himself. He patted his pockets until he found he cellphone.

"No." Tim's voice was hoarse. "No cops. Please Craig. No cops. I can't. Please." Tim leaned against the wall and Everett grabbed his arm before he collapsed completely.

Craig could barely look at Tim. His face was a mess. His left eye was black, his lip was split, and he was covered in dried blood from a bleeding nose. He was pale and barely able to stand on his own. Everett helped him over to the couch. Craig's hand shook, and he nearly dropped his phone. He'd totally forgotten he was holding it. He glanced down at his phone and shot a text to Alan.

At Everett's. Tim is here. He's been roughed up. Please come.

"No cops, Craig. Please." Tim's voice broke.

"Not cops. Alan." Craig stared at his phone and backed up another step. The room felt too small and it was too strange to be so close to Tim again. He'd thought he saw the last of him when he threw him out of the hotel.

Everett returned with a glass of water and a first aid kit tucked under his arm. He sat next to Tim and handed him a couple of painkillers and the water. Tim accepted both graciously. Once Tim swallowed them and drank his fill, Everett took the glass and set it aside. He rifled through the first aid kit. After he procured an antiseptic wipe, he carefully cupped Tim's chin with one hand.

"This might sting, but I want to make sure we clean you up okay?" Craig noticed a slight tremble in Everett's hands as he helped Tim. He hoped the sight of Tim hadn't brought back bad memories for Everett. Craig knew he'd been through something bad in his past. Craig put a hand on Everett's shoulder to comfort him.

Tim nodded. He winced a little when Everett cleaned the damage to his face, but other than that he kept his gaze focused on the floor.

"What happened, Tim?"

Tim glanced at Everett, but didn't say anything. He looked at Craig, but was barely able to maintain eye contact. "I fucked up. I fucked up so bad, Craig."

There was a time, months ago, when Craig would've killed to hear those words. Craig imagined a thousand different scenarios in which Tim would come crawling back, or would at least admit that he'd been wrong to leave Craig like that. But never in his wildest imagination did Craig picture this.

"What happened to you?" Craig's phone chimed with a text. It was Alan.

Be there in ten minutes. What's the apartment number?

Craig shot Alan a text letting him know that he'd come down to meet him at the front doors. He needed some space and possibly some fresh air. And Alan. He needed his boyfriend and his calming influence. The wine in Craig's stomach wasn't sitting well. He glanced at Everett and motioned to the door. Everett nodded, and Craig slipped out.

He didn't bother taking the elevator and headed for the stairs instead. He raced down them, desperate for some distance between him and Tim and whatever the fuck happened. Craig assumed it was that hot-headed Dom, boyfriend, whoever, that Craig had run into at the club.

Craig burst out the front doors and into the fresh air. He stood on the steps of his building, a four-story apartment that was on the older side of things, but the landlords kept it maintained. Craig took a seat on the steps. He wrapped his arms around his legs and set his chin on his knees. Maybe he should've listened to Tim when he'd sought him out. Was there a way Craig could've prevented all this from happening? Craig shook his head and reminded himself that Tim was the one who made the decision to leave. Anything that happened to him was a direct result of that decision. That didn't make it Tim's fault, and it certainly wasn't Craig's. He felt guilty anyway.

Craig looked at the time on his cellphone. Alan would be there any minute. Craig couldn't wait to throw his arms around him and breathe him in. He needed Alan. Everett was right. It was up to Craig to communicate better. He knew what he wanted, now all he had to do was reach out and ask for it.

Craig's mind started working out exactly what he wanted and how he was going to get it. Rehearsing conversations in his head was a good alternative to thinking about Tim. Craig was so immersed in his thoughts that he didn't notice Alan arrive until he heard his name called.

Craig lifted his gaze. His heart lightened when he saw Alan. Craig stood as Alan got to him. Alan pulled Craig into his arms and he kissed the side of Craig's head. "What's going on?" Alan asked.

Craig let his forehead rest against Alan's chest and he shut his eyes. "I was having a drink with Everett. We were talking about stuff and then someone knocked. Tim showed up here. He's all roughed up."

"Did you call the police?" Alan rubbed Craig's back as he spoke.

"He asked us not to." Craig clutched at Alan's shirt. "I hate this. I hate seeing him at all, but I hate seeing him like this even more. Even when I absolutely hated him I never wished anything like this on him. I'm not sure I can do this."

"Not sure you can do what?"

"Be there for him. I didn't want this to happen to him, I didn't. But he shows up here all fucked up and looking for help and I don't want to turn him away, but I don't have it in me to sit there and not wonder if there was something I could've done to prevent this. Maybe I should've listened to him when he came to me. I know it's not my fault, Alan, I know this, but I can't shake the guilt."

"Take a deep breath. It's okay." Alan stood there and let Craig collect himself for a minute before Alan insisted that they go upstairs to see what they could do about Tim. Alan took Craig's hand and didn't let go.

14
Alan

IT WASN'T A WONDER that Craig had been so shaken up when he arrived. One look at Tim's face and Alan was shaken as well, but under that was a layer of rage. He was angry at whoever did this to Tim and at Tim for showing up here and dumping his problems on Craig. He was mad at himself for being worried that Craig might want Tim back. Logic dictated that taking Tim back wasn't something Craig thought about doing, but somewhere inside Alan's mind there was a tiny irrational part of him that was worried sick that this was the beginning of the end.

It was irrational, but Alan couldn't stop comparing himself against Craig's ex. Tim and Craig had a history. They had a friendship that evolved into something more. Alan hadn't known Craig very long, they hadn't even—for lack of a better term—gone all the way, yet his feelings for Craig ran deeper than he'd ever anticipated. He hadn't said the words, but he'd wanted to. He wanted to kiss Craig until he was breathless. He wanted to touch every inch of him and possess him in every single way. Mind. Body. Soul. Alan was greedy where Craig was concerned. He wanted it all.

First Alan had to get him through this. Tim was a mess. He sat next to Everett, who gave Alan a polite nod. Everett whispered something to Tim. Tim nodded and Everett got up off the couch and signalled for Craig and Alan to follow him out into the hallway.

Craig kept himself glued to Alan's side. "What happened to him? Was it his boyfriend?"

Everett nodded. "It's a long story and it doesn't have a particularly happy ending."

"Give us the condensed version." Alan said. He made a mental note to revoke Paul's membership the minute he into the office. He also intended to send an email to the other clubs in the area.

"Paul saw Tim and Craig at a club a while back. Paul approached Tim on the sly and offered to train him to be a better Dom. That's how it started. It was never supposed to be a relationship, not at first, from what Tim told me. He wanted to please Craig. He knew something was off with the two of you and he didn't want to lose you."

Alan felt Craig flinch and he pulled him closer. He understood Tim's compulsion to do whatever was necessary to keep Craig. It was all he could think about.

"Paul told Tim the best way to learn to Dom was to be a sub." Everett stopped and chewed on his lip. He was clearly uncomfortable.

Craig dropped his gaze to the floor. "I know he cheated on me, Ev. It's okay. Can you just finish the story?"

Everett nodded and plunged into the rest of the tale. "By the time Tim left you Paul had him convinced that you didn't care about him because you never seemed to mind all the time he wasn't spending with you. He had Tim convinced that he'd be happier without you. Tim was clearly a verse, and you're all bottom," Everett's cheeks flushed, and he looked at Alan uneasily. "He was convinced that the two of you would never work out and that a clean break was what was best for you. He collared Tim and moved him into his house. He convinced Tim to quit his job because you could track him down there and he didn't want you making Tim feel bad. It went downhill from there."

"How bad?" Craig asked. Alan hated the thin, dejected tone of Craig's voice.

"Paul convinced him that he didn't have to find another job. He told Tim he'd take care of him. By the time Tim realized that Paul had stripped all his freedom away, he thought it was too late. He had no friends left. He had nowhere to go."

"How did he find out where I live?"

"He wouldn't tell me."

Alan felt Craig stiffen at his side. "I think I need to talk to Tim."

Craig stormed into Everett's apartment. He held onto Alan's hand the whole time. Alan loved that Craig needed him. It gave him hope that Craig wasn't about to leave him for a man who, for whatever reason, was so quick to cast him aside, even if he was manipulated into doing so. Alan couldn't imagine a world in which he'd willingly give Craig up.

They stood across the room from Tim, who still sat in the recliner. He had a blanket wrapped around his shoulders and his face was turning a grotesque shade of purple around his eye.

Craig wasted no time jumping into his line of questioning. “How did you know where I lived? Why did you come here? Why were you at my job?”

Tim looked up at Craig and Alan saw how empty and sad and broken the man was. “I didn’t know what I was getting into until it was too late. I knew where you lived because I looked for you. I looked for you and you moved. I had to ask around, but eventually I found out that you moved into this building.” Tim shrugged. “Your name is on the intercom at the main doors. That’s how I found your apartment number. I slipped in when another tenant opened the doors.”

Craig gripped Alan’s hand tighter. “Why did you come here? I don’t get it. You fucking vanished. Then I see you in the club and suddenly you’re desperate to find me.”

Tim’s eyes started to water, and he swiped at the tears. “Paul was mad about that. He was mad that you got him in trouble at the club. He was embarrassed… and I made it worse. I always thought he was right. That you were okay with how things went down with us. That it was better. But then I saw you in the club and I saw how much I hurt you. I was angry. I came here to try and talk to you, to explain what happened. I don’t blame you for not listening, but I was mad. I was mad about everything. I called him out for manipulating me.”

“Was that all he was mad about?” Alan raised an eyebrow.

He didn't know Tim at all, but he sensed that there was something he was leaving out.

Tim swallowed and shook his head.

"What else was he mad about, Tim?" Craig asked, his voice barely audible.

Tim looked at the floor. "When I saw you at the club . . . he knew. He saw it written all over my face."

"Saw what?" Alan asked the question he knew Craig was too afraid to. It wasn't like Alan didn't know the answer. Any fool could see that Tim was still in love with Craig. It was written all over his face. It was apparent in the way he carried himself, so full of regret and shame and self hatred, that Tim still carried a torch for the man he'd wronged.

Then Tim opened his mouth and Alan's worst nightmare came true.

"He knew I was still in love with you."

There was dead silence for a moment, then Craig let out a shaky breath. "Call your brother. You can stay here with Everett until he comes and gets you, or you can stay in my apartment and I'll stay with Alan. I think, given the circumstances, that it's best if you leave town. Go stay with your family, they'll support you and help you through this. I can't, I won't, and I don't want to."

Tim flinched as if he'd been slapped.

"You left me for whatever reason, I don't even care anymore. I'll help you get away from Paul because he's bad news, but that's it. I'm not your shoulder to lean on. I'm not the light at the end of your tunnel. I'm just a guy you used to know who is doing you one last favor." Craig looked at Alan. "Can we go? I need . . . I can't be here anymore."

Alan nodded. Even though Craig had laid down the law with Tim and outright rejected him, it hardly felt like a victory. Once they were out in the hallway, Craig looked up at Alan. "You don't mind if I stay with you, do you?"

Alan wrapped his arm around Craig's shoulders. He wanted to wrap Craig up in his arms and hold him until the intense unease fled his body. "Let's pack you a bag. You can stay for as long as you need to." He wanted to tell Craig that he could stay with him forever if he chose to, but now wasn't the moment for grand declarations of love. That would come later, because Alan was going to tell Craig how he felt about him.

From the moment he'd first laid eyes on Craig, he was struck. Then he touched him, held him, and talked to him. The more he was around Craig the more he realized that he didn't want to let him go. He loved him. Alan knew that with the sale of the club looming on the horizon, that his future was a little uncertain, but he'd do anything he could to make sure Craig was in it.

Craig was subdued as he packed a bag. Alan stayed close, but didn't press him for conversation. They stopped by Everett's quickly to thank him for helping Tim. Alan watched as Everett wrapped his gangly arms around Craig and pulled him into a hug. Everett whispered something in Craig's ear, then patted him on the back. He looked at Alan and nodded, then disappeared back into his apartment.

Alan led Craig to his car. Craig reached out and put his hand on Alan's thigh, but stayed quiet. Alan guessed that Craig was going to need some time and space to process everything he'd learned. His relationship with Tim might've been doomed, but the manipulation from Paul was a revelation of sorts and Alan wondered how Craig would handle it.

Craig thumped his head against the headrest. "I have to work tomorrow."

Alan glanced at Craig. "Why don't you take some time off? You can stay with me."

"I don't want to be your tag-a-long while you work at the club. I'll feel pathetic."

"I'll work from home. What I can't do from home, I can delegate."

A minute later Craig was on the phone with his Uncle. "Yeah, uh, Uncle Hank," Craig exhaled a shaky breath. "I need time off. Yeah, uh, Tim showed up. No. Of course not." Absolute disgust filled Craig's voice. "I'm staying with Alan for a couple of days." Pause. "I promise to fill you in later." Pause. "Yeah, he will, don't worry."

Another pause made Alan wish he could hear both sides of the conversation.

"Yeah, we can do that." Craig looked at Alan. "Uncle Hank wants to have dinner with us in a few days." Craig pressed the phone against his chest so his uncle wouldn't be able to hear. "He's worried about me."

"It's no problem, Craig."

Craig nodded then put the phone back to his ear. "I'll call you in a few days and we'll set something up, okay." Craig exhaled and leaned against the headrest and closed his eyes. "I will Uncle Hank. You too." Craig ended the call and dropped his hands into his lap. He kept his eyes shut and Alan took that as a sign that he needed a few minutes of quiet.

They didn't speak again until Craig walked through Alan's front door. Craig shifted his bag from one hand to the other and toed his shoes off before looking at Alan. "I'm going to head upstairs, if that's okay."

Alan resisted the urge to wrap his arms around Craig. He wanted to touch him, soothe him, and make it all better. Instead, Alan nodded. "Put your stuff in my room and make yourself at home. I'll be up in a little while to check on you, okay?"

Craig nodded. Alan thought he was going to walk away, but Craig came closer. He put his free hand on Alan's shoulder, then rose and kissed him on the cheek. "Thank you."

Alan followed him to the stairs and watched Craig as he climbed them. He hated to see Craig like this. Alan shook his head and wandered into the kitchen. He tried to stop his imagination from working overtime, but even as he put the kettle on to boil water for hot chocolate, he couldn't stop thinking about Craig. The night he met him, he knew Craig had some sort of history with Tim or Paul, but he didn't know what. Now that he knew the whole truth, Alan couldn't stop picturing Craig and how ruined he must've been when Tim left.

When Alan met Craig there had been a sadness in his eyes, likely the lingering effects of Tim's betrayal. Slowly, as he got to know Craig, it seemed to ease. It hadn't totally vanished yet, and that bothered Alan. More than anything he wanted to make Craig happy. He wanted to chase the shadows out of his eyes.

Alan's hand shook a little as he stirred the cup of cocoa for Craig. He wasn't sure how to proceed. He could bring Craig a cup of hot chocolate and suggest they watch a movie. He could see if Craig wanted him to order dinner or if he felt up to cooking with Alan. They'd both enjoyed the time they spent together in the kitchen. Alan wasn't used to feeling so helpless. With an ache in his heart, Alan carried the cocoa upstairs.

He almost walked into his bedroom unannounced, but stopped at the last moment and knocked. "Craig. I'm coming in, okay."

There was no response. Alan sighed and pushed the door open.

"I brought some hot chocolate." Alan heard his voice trail off when he spotted Craig.

Craig. Naked and kneeling. His arms were clasped behind his back. His head was bowed. Alan's inner Dom instantly woke up and everything clicked into place. His boy needed something that only his Daddy could give him. Alan set the cup on the dresser and let himself stare at Craig—his boy—for a minute.

Alan's throat tightened, his pulse raced, and his dick hardened in his pants. He adjusted himself as he raked his gaze down the graceful curve of Craig's spine. He loved his perfect ass, round and firm Alan's cock twitched when he wondered how tight Craig would be.

Alan walked in a slow circle around Craig. He kept his hands to himself for now as he gathered his control. His boy was so beautiful. There was an air of calm that Craig hadn't had downstairs. He was calmer, but Alan saw the tension in his neck and shoulders. He saw the way Craig had to force himself to breathe evenly.

Alan reached out and brushed his fingers through Craig's hair. "Tell me what you need, boy."

Craig's shoulders dropped a little as some of the tension in his muscles fled. "I need you, Daddy."

Alan smiled a little even though he really wanted to lift Craig into his arms and kiss him senseless. There would be time for that later. Instead, Alan let his fingers slide over Craig's scalp. He relished the way his boy shivered a little. "You need me, Little One?"

"Yes, Daddy." Craig's voice was soft and steady. Without being prompted to, Craig lifted his gaze to find Alan's. Where Alan expected to see the familiar shadows of sadness, he saw only adoration. He expected to hear hesitant words, but instead was floored by conviction. "I need you. I need you to make me yours, Daddy. I've wanted to belong to you since that first night."

Alan could scarcely breathe. He'd been so unsure of himself where Craig was concerned that he'd held back. He hadn't wanted to push too hard too soon despite his urge to own him completely, and here was Craig; kneeling and begging for the very thing Alan wanted most.

Alan smiled down at Craig and cupped his cheek. He let his thumb glide over Craig's cheekbone. Reluctantly, he pulled his hand away and crossed the room. Despite telling himself that he hadn't expected to use this any time soon, he'd still bought it *just in case.* Alan wanted to laugh at his own ignorance. Now was the time for absolute honesty. He'd wanted this from the moment Craig went to his knees.

He opened the top drawer of his dresser and opened a

box that he'd stashed inside. He retrieved the contents and went back to Craig. He kept the item behind his back so Craig couldn't see it.

Alan stroked the curve of Craig's jaw with his fingertips. "You are mine. The minute you knelt, we connected. From that first touch, I was hooked. You're mine and I'm not ever going to let you go." Alan showed Craig the item he'd hidden behind his back and Craig's eyes widened.

"Is that?" Craig swallowed. Anticipation flickered in his eyes and Alan didn't hide his smile.

"Yes, Little One. It is, and I got it especially for you. I'm going to be completely honest with you." Alan's fingers slid over the smooth black leather of the collar and he unfastened the buckle. "This is a collar and I want you to wear it. I want to be your Daddy. I want to own you and use you and fuck you until you're boneless. But I'm greedy, because I also want to be your lover. I want to hold you and caress you and make love to you. I'm selfish and I want you all to myself. I want to cook dinner with you, watch movies with you, travel with you. I want to be your Daddy, your lover, and your boyfriend. I want to be your everything, Craig." Alan held his breath and the world seemed to stop spinning for a moment. Maybe it faded away completely because there was only Alan and Craig. Alan took a breath. "Will you be my everything, Little One?"

"Yes, Daddy." Those words were the single most glorious sounds that Alan had ever heard.

Alan bent and buckled the collar around Craig's neck. He didn't miss the way Craig's Adam's apple bobbed when he swallowed, or the little hitch in his breath when Alan's fingers skimmed across his throat and up to his chin. He tipped Craig's head up. God, he was perfect. His full lips, parted so he could pant, though he was almost breathless at that point. Lust-filled eyes framed by dark lashes stared up at him.

Unable to resist him, Alan captured Craig's mouth. With a little moan that sounded a lot like relief and consuming desire all wrapped up in one tiny package, Craig submitted to Alan as he parted his lips and slid his tongue into Craig's mouth.

Their kiss was all softness with an undercurrent of scorching heat and barely controlled need. Alan needed Craig like he needed air. He needed to own him and consume him and control him in a way that he hadn't needed anyone in a long time. Craig was wearing his collar and it was the most glorious sight in the world and Alan was going to show him what it meant to belong to him completely.

Alan straightened his back, rolled his shoulders, and his Dom voice rolled out, smooth as silk and firm like steel. "Stand up, Sweetheart."

15
Craig

HOLYSHITHOLYSHITHOLYSHITHOLYSHIT. ***YES!*** CRAIG TRIED to stop his mind from going a million miles an hour, but between Alan's words, the feel of the smooth leather around his throat, and that soul-destroying kiss, Craig was already about to blow apart at the seams. Then Alan whipped out his Daddy voice and Craig nearly came on the spot.

As graceful as he could manage, he got to his feet. He knew he should look down, but he wasn't able to take his eyes off Alan. His Dom. His Daddy. No, not just that. Alan was his everything and he was perfect. From the crows feet at the corner of his eyes down to the fuzzy patch of hair on his chest. There wasn't an inch of the man that Craig didn't appreciate the fuck out of.

"Climb onto the bed. Kneel in the center."

Craig didn't trust himself to speak. His entire body was pulled tight with anticipation. He hurried over to the bed.

Fuck being graceful, he wasn't showing off for anyone and Alan's dark chuckle indicated that he enjoyed Craig's enthusiasm. He knelt in the center of the bed and waited. And waited. Behind him he heard noises and he nearly turned around to see what Alan was doing, but he stopped himself. He wanted to please Alan. He wanted to be perfect for him.

Craig closed his eyes and did his best to be patient.

"Lean forward. Put your cheek on the mattress. Ass in the air."

God his voice sounded good. There was a ferocious intensity that Craig hadn't ever heard from Alan. His cock liked it. Slowly, obediently, Craig lowered himself until his cheek was pressed against the mattress. He took a deep breath and it shuddered out of him when Alan reached over and arranged his arms so they were stretched out down his sides.

Cold leather wrapped around one wrist. Then the other. "Do you remember your safe word, Little One?"

Craig didn't recognize his own voice when he spoke. He sounded so far gone already, so breathy and thin, yet wound so tight and Alan hadn't even done anything yet. "Red, Daddy."

Alan smoothed his hand over Craig's back. He caressed the curve of his ass. "Good Boy." Then Alan's touch was gone. Without it, Craig felt naked... well, metaphorically naked. He was already literally naked except for his collar and the cuffs Alan had put around his wrists. Alan put cuffs around Craig's thighs then secured them to the cuffs around his wrists. The position he was in was a little humiliating, but his dick had no complaints. With his arms at his sides secured to his thighs, his face down, ass up, legs spread, Alan had full access. Craig bit back a moan.

For a few minutes, Alan seemed content to pet him. He stroked his hands over every exposed inch of Craig's body. Powerful hands caressed every curve, every muscle down his back. His fingertips grazed over every vertebra then the crease of his ass as Alan caressed it. He kept telling Craig how perfect he was. How beautiful he looked. Craig's chest tightened with every ounce of praise.

He'd wanted to be those things for Alan. He wanted to be them so bad he ached. He was tired of trying and failing and never being enough for anyone. But here, on Alan's bed, with the comfort of his collar around his neck, the feel of Alan's hands on him, and the sound of his voice singing Craig's praises over and over, Craig believed everything Alan was saying.

"That's it, Little One. You're so nice and relaxed now." Alan practically purred as his hands once again smoothed down Craig's ass. Alan's hand travelled lower. Craig choked off a startled sound that morphed into a moan when Alan's fingers cupped his balls. Craig moaned, and Alan chuckled. Then something wrapped around the base of his cock and around his balls and tightened. Craig gasped and wriggled his fingers looking for something to grab onto. "Holy shit, Daddy." Craig panted, and his fingers scrabbled unsuccessfully for something to grip onto. "Is that..."

"It's a little toy to help you. You're so beautiful when you're eager, but I don't want you coming too soon."

Craig didn't like the sound of that. Not really. Even though he swore the room heated five degrees and his balls tightened. Okay, so he was, in fact, fighting the urge to roll his eyes into the back of his head and float away with all the ideas that flashed through his mind of what Alan could possibly have in store for him.

Craig nearly leapt out of his skin when a breath of warm air washed over his hole.

"I love how your body responds to me, Little One." Alan stroked his thumb down the crease of Craig's ass, then back up again. Craig grunted when the thumb stopped and lightly pressed against his pucker. He clamped his eyes shut and tried to steady his breathing. Alan had been a genius to put the cock ring on him. He'd have blown his load already for sure, but he couldn't. He was trapped on the edge of ecstasy and Alan was determined to make him ride it for as long as possible, because the next thing he knew, the thumb disappeared. Craig heard something open. He jerked when a well lubed finger swirled around his hole, then gently pressed inside.

"Ung. Fuck." Craig wanted to bury his face into the mattress, bite a pillow, maybe scream or at least rock back and fuck himself on that one finger, but Alan's other hand pressed down on the curve of his ass, keeping him still.

"That's right. Let me hear all those glorious sounds. I want to hear you fall apart." Alan slowly worked in a second finger as Craig chanted a string of expletives. Alan chuckled darkly. "If you could see how beautiful you look, Sweetheart." Alan's hand stroked across Craig's lower back and Craig bit his lip. "You're trying so hard not to fall apart." Alan's voice was soothing. It slid under Craig's skin and made him want to let go for Alan. Craig exhaled and closed his eyes and he swore he heard Alan purr.

Craig jerked a little when Alan slid his finger out. He felt empty, voided, bereft even. His eyes snapped open and he caught sight of Alan, who smiled a sweet sort of smile that Craig had never seen before. "Relax. It's okay. I've got you."

Craig felt the words more than he heard them. They uncoiled something inside him and he felt the last bit of tension leave his shoulders. Alan had him. Alan was there, and Craig trusted him like he'd never trusted anyone, because Alan hadn't ever pushed for anything. He never hinted that he wanted more. He never did anything but be there for Craig and support him and believe that he was enough.

He was enough.

He was enough, and Alan had him and he let go. For the first time, maybe ever, Craig let go for real. He relaxed, and Alan smoothed his powerful hands over Craig's back. Then something hard and slick pressed at his entrance. Craig didn't need to be told what to do, he let Alan work the plug inside him because he was Alan's and Alan was his. Alan swore he had him so Craig submitted to his Daddy. His Dom. His lover and boyfriend. His everything.

The plug was bigger than Craig was used to and it stretched and stung a little, even though Alan worked it in slowly. Alan never stopped touching him, petting him. He didn't stop speaking to him either. Craig's world had shrunk down to contain only Alan. He surrounded him with his voice and his touch and the scent of him that clung to the bed.

When the plug was fully seated Alan gave it a sharp smack.

Craig yelped and jerked in his bindings. The smack made a jolt of electricity shoot straight through Craig, right from his ass to the top of his head and exploding outward like a firework. Then Alan's hands stroked lower. He knelt on the bed, one hand slid up Craig's spine and came to rest at the back of his neck. His thumb stroked along Craig's heated skin and Alan's warmth blanketed him as he wrapped his other hand around Craig's throbbing cock.

"Oh god. Yes. Please." Craig begged, for what exactly, he didn't know. But he needed… something. Everything. Alan. He needed Alan. He needed to make him happy. He needed to be everything Alan needed. "Please. Fuck. God." Craig swore as Alan slowly jacked him. His balls tightened, but couldn't release and his entire body got hotter, sweatier, needier. He practically burned with the desire for Alan to rip the plug from his ass and take him, fuck him, fill him and mark him and make him his for real.

"What is it, Sweetheart?"

Alan knew what he needed. There was no way he didn't, not when Craig's mouth was hanging halfway open and he was panting and so fucking turned on he couldn't barely think. But Alan wanted the words so Craig gave them to him.

"I need… you. I need you. So much." And then the words came sliding out of Craig's mouth like the answer to a prayer. "Daddy. I need you."

He didn't miss the way Alan's breath hitched, or the way his fingers tightened on his cock. "You have me, Little One. You do. You know that. I'm yours and you're mine."

Alan moved away, and Craig didn't bother tracking his

movements and worrying about where he was going and what he was going to do. It didn't matter. Alan was there. His. Everything. Craig waited quietly, not moving a muscle. Then Alan was back and something soft brushed down his spine, slowly. The softness caressed each vertebrae and Craig shuddered. It was so slow, and it felt so good, so amazing, that it felt almost like torture. The touch was there, but almost not and it made him squirm. He jumped and barked out in surprise when the softness continued down the crease of his ass and underneath him. He choked back a moan when the softness licked at his balls. Then it vanished, and Craig's nerves chased the phantoms of its touch.

Alan continued to touch him everywhere. With soft things and prickly things and things that felt slightly scratchy, but mostly amazing on his now super sensitive skin. His brain sparked with white-hot awareness of everything that touched him. The soft scratch of the comforter when he shifted even a little. The glide of precum as it beaded on his engorged cock. Even the feel of his own panting breaths passing over his lips was pulling him farther apart and somehow putting him back together.

Then Craig was begging. "Alan. Please." Alan. Not Daddy or Sir or anything else. Alan. He needed Alan. Because though he was his Dom. His Daddy. His Sir. He was first, last, and always his lover. His everything. "Alan. Please." Craig panted again as he clenched and unclenched his fists. "I need you. Please. God. Fuck me."

Alan stroked a hand down the center of Craig's spine, a move that Craig guessed was becoming Alan's favorite. The reason eluded Craig. But that didn't matter, because Alan unfastened Craig's arms. Craig didn't move, not yet. Alan was touching him. Stroking his hands up the sides of Craig's thighs. Then down his ass. Alan's thumbs grazed the crease and Craig shuddered with anticipation as he exhaled.

Alan plucked at the plug that still sat in Craig's ass. Craig twitched as a million fireworks of pleasure shot off inside him. His desperate cock twitched, but didn't shoot. "Ung. Fuck. Please." Craig panted and finally forced his eyes to open. Alan was gazing at him and the expression on his face made Craig light up on the inside. So much lust. So much adoration. So many emotions that Craig couldn't put a name to and they were all focused on him. Him. "Please." Craig said as he gave his ass a little wiggle. He'd intended the word to be playful, but he'd passed urgency a long time ago and his entire body practically vibrated with need.

Alan stripped out of his clothes—fucking finally—and above the sound of Craig's harsh breathing he heard the crinkle of a condom wrapper. Alan's eyes were hooded, and Craig could almost see the lust radiate off his skin. Alan took hold of the base of the plug and it made a lewd squelching noise when he eased it out.

The bed dipped a little and Craig pulled his arms up and stretched them out in front of himself as Alan climbed up behind him. Craig liked that Alan took a moment to smooth his hands up Craig's sides. His cock nestled in the crease of Craig's ass and Alan leaned forward. His fingers brushed the back of Craig's neck, then tickled down his spine.

He loved how silent the room was. The only sounds Craig

heard were the pounding of his heart, his ragged breathing, and Alan's gentle hum of appreciation as he gripped his cock and pressed it against Craig's entrance.

Alan slid into Craig's boneless body with one long steady push.

"Fuck." Alan's grip on Craig's hips tightened. He stayed still for a moment. Craig felt Alan's heavy gaze on him. Craig sighed and rocked back a little.

"So good. You feel, oh shit," a jolt of pleasure rocketed through Craig and he twitched. His fingers gripped into the comforter until he was clenching his fists around handfuls of fabric. "Oh god. Amazing. So fucking amazing."

Alan swivelled his hips and the grinding motion had Craig panting and forcing his ass back into Alan. The sound of Alan's groan was deep and thrilling and knowing that he made Alan make such a primitive and guttural sound did something to Craig's insides.

"You're so fucking hot. Tight. Fuuuuck." Alan said as he pulled back until only the head of his cock was still inside Craig. Then he slammed home and Craig pushed himself up on his elbows.

Alan leaned down, his weight and warmth pressed into Craig's back. He mouthed the shell of Craig's ear. "You're beautiful. You're so fucking beautiful, Sweetheart." Alan wrapped an arm around Craig's torso. It looped under one of Craig's arms and his hand cupped the opposite shoulder.

Alan fucked him with slow steady strokes that lit him up from the inside. Each lazy kiss on his neck and shoulder had his cock twitching, weeping, practically begging for release.

Then Alan's grip on Craig's shoulder tightened. He stopped thrusting long enough to slowly pull Craig toward him. Then Craig was kneeling on the bed. He was upright, and Alan was behind him. Alan wrapped his other arm around Craig's waist. The hand that was on his shoulder blazed a trail of fire up his neck, and Alan turned Craig's head. The kiss was passionate and only slightly awkward and all kinds of hot. Alan was inside him. Around him. Under his skin and in his heart.

The kiss broke apart. Craig leaned his head back against Alan, who buried his face in the crook of Craig's neck. His arms tightened around Craig. He held him tight, but careful, as if he were something precious. Something to be treasured. Craig almost said the words right then, but he didn't want the first time he told Alan he loved him to be in the middle of sex. He wanted Alan to believe that the words came from his heart, and were not spoken hastily, in the middle of passion.

No longer able to stay upright, Craig lowered himself to the bed. He pressed the side of his face into the mattress. Alan put a hand on his back, between his shoulder blades, the other hand grabbed a handful of ass and Alan thrust inside him. He fucked him hard and relentless, his cock endlessly pressed against Craig's prostate. A string of sounds that weren't quite words but still managed to sound like begging poured out of Craig as the need to fall apart rumbled through him like a freight train with failed brakes.

Alan leaned down. He braced one hand next to Craig's head, the other slid across Craig's stomach, then down. He removed the cock ring, then slammed into Craig. Craig cried out as he came and splattered the bed with his cum.

Alan pulled out and Craig fell to the mattress. He turned his head in time to see Alan rip the condom off. He threw his head back and gripped his cock. He jacked once, twice, then shot all over Craig's back. The look of absolute bliss on Alan's face made Craig feel giddy light headed.

Alan collapsed on top of Craig. Alan was heavy, but warm and he didn't even mind the sticky mess on his back, or his chest. After a moment, Alan shifted a bit to the right so he wasn't totally squishing Craig. Craig laid there and enjoyed the floaty feeling that turned his brain to mush. He barely registered the hot puffs of air on the back of his neck, or the gliding fingers that made the hair on his arm stand on end. Soft lips brushed against his shoulder as he dropped off to sleep.

The first thing that Craig noticed when he woke was Alan's heartbeat thumping in his ear. He was sprawled over top of Alan. His head rested on Alan's chest, his arm was thrown across Alan's stomach and their legs were tangled together. Familiar fingers stroked his scalp.

"Hey." Alan whispered. "You're back."

"Mmmm." Craig was still boneless and completely satisfied. "That was awesome." He hated that he wasn't articulate, but awesome was the best he could do with his sleep-addled, post-orgasm brain.

Alan pressed a kiss to the top of Craig's head. "You know," Alan sounded a little hesitant to speak, so Craig stayed quiet and waited for him to continue. "When Mike left I didn't know who I was for a while after. I was a Dom without a sub and then, after a while, I didn't feel like a Dom at all. I couldn't connect with anyone. I couldn't give anyone what they needed. I felt like a complete failure. I failed Mike. I failed all those subs that I didn't really connect with."

Alan stroked his hand up and down Craig's side. "And then you walked into my club, we connected, and you needed something and I fucking prayed that I could be the something you needed. It was terrifying, Craig. Absolutely terrifying to hope that I could be enough for you."

Craig's breath caught, and he propped himself up on his elbow so he could look at Alan. With his free hand he cupped Alan's cheek. "I'm not hardcore. I never was and that's why it never worked with Tim. When I met you, I wanted you. I wanted to be yours from that first moment. For a long time, I was convinced that I'd never be enough for anyone because I thought Tim was perfect for me and I wasn't enough for him."

Alan looked horrified in one moment and in the next he looked at Craig with adoration so absolute it made his insides quake. "You're enough. You're so much more than enough."

Craig leaned down and kissed Alan. He smiled against Alan's mouth. "I know." Craig pulled back and let himself drown a little in Alan's soft blue eyes. "I love you, Alan."

Alan wrapped his arms around Craig and hauled him up so that Craig was sprawled out on top of Alan. "I love you, too."

Craig grinned, then kissed him. It was soft and slow and hot and so full of passion and heat and Alan and everything that Craig thought he might burst with happiness. Then Alan flipped him over and fucked him into oblivion and he did burst, all over the mattress, again.

* * *

"You don't have to do this, you know." Alan reassured Craig as they headed toward the living room where Craig had asked Tim to wait.

"I think I might. Not for him. For me." Craig squeezed Alan's hand. "Thank you for being with me, though. I know I couldn't do this alone."

"There's nowhere else I'd rather be." Alan shot a glance in the direction of the living room. "I can ask him to leave if you want."

"No. I'm glad he showed up, sort of. Maybe." Craig exhaled then did his best to steady his nerves. "Let's get this over with."

Craig took a deep breath as Alan slid his arm around Craig's waist and pulled him close. It felt like a territorial maneuver on Alan's part, but Craig didn't mind. The fact that Alan was laying claim to him in front of Tim made his heart sing. In the days since Craig had gone home with Alan they'd fallen into a lovely routine of absolute domestic bliss.

Domestic bliss that was interrupted this morning when Tim showed up unannounced, with a huge apology for using the internet to track down Alan's home address. Tim's brother was waiting down the street at a little cafe and he'd promised not to stay long. Craig asked for five minutes to gather himself and those five minutes were up.

Tim was a shy lump with slumped shoulders sitting in the center of Alan's couch. When Craig and Alan walked into the room, Tim didn't straighten. He looked at Craig, then Alan, and he gave them a little nod before dropping his gaze again.

Craig dropped into the recliner. Alan perched on the arm next to him and kept a hand on his back. He tucked his hand under Craig's shirt and his thumb stroked back and forth. Craig was grateful for the contact. Sitting across from Tim and was a surreal experience. For a long time, he'd had conversations in his head. He rehearsed a thousand different speeches but now he had no words. There was nothing he really wanted to say to Tim.

Tim spoke first. He lifted his head and made eye contact with Craig. "I'm sorry. I'm so fucking sorry, Craig."

Craig furrowed his brow. The bruises had really set in over the past couple of days and his face was a mixture of purple, black and green around his left eye, but the swelling had gone down. "I always thought that I'd want an apology from you Tim, but I don't. I'm not heartbroken anymore. I'm not mad anymore. I'm sorry you got yourself hurt." Craig took a breath and wrapped his arm around Alan. "The way you left me was cruel, Tim. It was heartless, and it fucked me up for a long time, but it brought Alan and I together. I'm not about to thank you or fall at your feet for screwing me over, no matter how great I have it now, it still hurt. Go home, Tim. Go home to your family and get your head on straight. That's all I want."

Tim sighed. "I didn't mean for things to happen they way they did, you know. When I met Paul, he told me that he could tell that we weren't happy together." Tim raised his gaze and Craig saw the same sort of sadness that long ago haunted his own gaze every time he looked in the mirror. "We weren't going to make it. You know that. But I wanted us to make it. I really did." Tim took a deep breath. He wrung his hands in his lap. His left leg bounced, tell-tale sign that Tim was nervous. "He said that he could help me. But what he did wasn't help. It was control and manipulation and abuse."

Craig cocked his head to the side and Tim shrugged.

"I talked to Everett a lot the past couple of days. He helped me sort of put things in perspective. Or start to at least." Tim wiped an errant tear. "I pushed you. I always pushed you for more and I shouldn't have, not the way I did. I wish I could say that Everett taught me that, but it was Paul." Tim shrugged, and Craig thought he saw him shudder. "Some things you learn first hand." Tim's phone chimed. He looked at the screen and stood. "Greg is in the driveway. He wants to get going." Tim shoved his phone back in his pocket.

"I'll walk you out." Alan offered.

Tim looked down at Craig. Craig had no desire to stand up and make a grand declaration of wanting to be friends one day, or exchanging pleasantries about keeping in touch. He wouldn't mean any of it anyway, so he stuck with the truth.

"Bye, Tim. Take care of yourself. Okay?"

Tim nodded and shoved his hands in his pockets. "Okay."

He watched Tim and Alan leave the room, then collapsed into the chair as if he'd deflated. He closed his eyes and listened as the front door opened, then closed. Gravel crunched, and Tim was gone. Probably forever this time.

Alan returned to Craig a moment later. He sat on the coffee table and leaned forward so he could grab Craig's hands. "You okay? Do you need anything?"

Craig cracked an eye open and smiled at Alan. "The only thing I need is you."

Alan smiled then tugged Craig to his feet and took him upstairs.

EPILOGUE
Craig

Four Months Later

AFTER TWO MONTHS OF living out in a hotel, it was strange to wake up back in Alan's bedroom. Alan had taken the job Craig's Uncle Hank offered him. Alan was now in charge of turning around some of the newly acquired hotels. Hank, knowing that Alan would turn down any job that took him away from Craig, offered Craig a new job. Craig received a fancy raise and was now in charge of retraining all the staff in the hotel. This was the first weekend they'd been home in two months.

Craig slid into a shiny black shirt and a pair of black pants. It was the same outfit he'd worn that first night he met Alan and it seemed fitting to wear it tonight to the grand re-opening of the club. The sale had gone off without a hitch and the renovations completed. Steve was ready to launch his brand new kink club.

Craig turned to Alan, who sat on the bed to put his socks on. "How's Steve doing anyway?"

"He's still pissed that Matt put his notice in. I guess he promised him everything short of the moon to try and convince him to stay, but Matt insisted that it was time to move on."

Craig frowned. "Seems like a shit thing to do, you know. Matt was an experienced waiter and he quits just when Steve expands his business."

Alan shrugged. "I'm sure Matt had his reasons." He stood and swept Craig into his arms. Craig wriggled a little in a half-hearted attempt to escape. "We can't be late. Steve will kill us."

Alan's lips kissed their way up the side of Craig's neck. "It would be worth it." Alan whispered in Craig's ear.

Craig laughed and pushed Alan away. "You only say that because Steve doesn't scare you."

Alan barked out a laugh. "And he scares you?"

Craig's eyes widened. "Yes. Have you not seen him? He's huge. His arms are the size of my thighs and his switch is always flipped to super-dom or something. He's frightening."

Alan laughed about Craig's super-dom comment all the way to the club and only promised not to tell Steve when Craig threatened to withhold sex. Alan and Craig walked into the club which had already amassed a decent sized crowd. "Are you nervous? I know you don't really like these places."

Craig shrugged. "I'm fine. It's not like you're going to ask me to kneel naked at your feet all night or suck your dick in front of everyone."

Alan leaned over and kissed Craig's temple. They'd spent

a lot of time working through Craig's hang-ups, but some of them still lingered. He'd probably never be comfortable doing a scene in a club, but they weren't here for that. They were here for Steve, who stormed over. He had a smile plastered on his face, but Craig could tell that something was off.

When Steve reached them, he nodded his head toward an empty table that had a big 'reserved' sign on it. Steve dropped into a chair. Alan and Craig sat across from him.

"What's wrong?" Alan glanced around. Everyone was mingling, smiling, eating, and generally having a great time.

Steve scrubbed his face with his hands. "Matt was here. Do you know why he quit?"

Alan shrugged. "Should I?"

Steve shook his head. "He showed up here wearing these tiny little shorts and a whole lot of fucking glitter and he fucking threw himself at me. He quit the restaurant because he knows I have more sense than to fuck my employees."

Craig whistled. "Shit. I take it his advances didn't go over too well?"

"He threw himself at me in front of a room full of people. He walked right up to me and made a blatant pass at me."

Craig looked at Alan. Alan had a strange look on his face. "You make it sound like that's a bad thing. I've told you that he's had a thing for you since you hired him."

"I don't fuck my employees."

"But he's not your employee."

Craig's gaze alternated between Steve and Alan and he watched them do that annoying thing where they stared at each other and had an entire conversation that he wasn't privy to because he didn't speak their secret, silent, BFF-mind-meld-lingo or whatever it was that enabled them to do that.

Steve shrugged, and Craig knew that part of the conversation was over. "I have to check on things in the kitchen. Mingle. Have fun. Eat whatever you want, it's all on the house." When Steve left the table he seemed slightly calmer, but maybe a little sadder, too.

"Is he okay?" Craig asked Alan.

Alan shrugged. "I don't know. I think he knows he fucked up. Whether he'll admit it or not-which he won't, he's had a soft spot for Matt since the day he hired him. I think he's sad Matt won't be working for him, but I think it's more than that."

Craig knew better than to try and pry too deep into what Alan knew about Steve. The two friends went back a long way and while he'd share stories from their glory days, this was different. This was too personal.

Craig shoved his chair a little closer to Alan's. He rested his head on Alan's arm and entwined their fingers. "I may not like coming to clubs, but I'm glad I walked into yours."

"It's a shame you couldn't convince your friend Everett to come. He'd be popular."

Craig laughed and rolled his eyes. "I tried, but getting that guy to leave his apartment is like trying to scrape old gum off the bottom of a theatre seat." Craig cringed at the visual he gave himself. "Okay, that was a gross example, but you get my point."

"Do you think he's agoraphobic or something? Anxiety maybe?" Alan asked.

"Nah." Craig said. "He leaves when he has a good reason to leave and he never seems bothered by it. But he's more comfortable at home." Craig sighed. "Speaking of home…"

"Yes, Little One?"

Craig nestled up against Alan. "I bought a new can of shaving cream and a straight razor."

Alan arched an eyebrow, but said nothing.

"You did mention shaving me once, did you not?"

Alan's eyes sparkled with interest. "Get your coat, Little One. We're leaving."

"Yes, Daddy."

* * *

"I think you should sit down for this, Little One," Alan said as he placed a chair near the counter in the spacious bathroom. "You're practically vibrating, and you haven't even undressed yet."

Craig offered him a sly smile. "I am a little excited," he admitted. When Alan scoffed Craig rolled his eyes. "Okay. I'm like a little kid on Christmas morning."

Alan filled a basin with hot water and got a few towels ready.

"I've wanted to do this for a long time." Alan said as he approached Craig and put his hands on Craig's hips. He slid his hands up Craig's body, taking the shiny black shirt up his torso. Craig raised his arms and Alan stripped the shirt off him then tossed it aside. Alan's hands stroked Craig's naked chest. Even after months of being together, Alan never seemed to get enough of Craig. Then Alan undid Craig's pants and slowly removed them.

"I've wanted this for a long time, too, Daddy. I've pictured it a million times since you mentioned it." He really had. Ever since Alan tied him to a chair and teased him with filthy words the image of Alan shaving him wouldn't leave his mind. Craig couldn't even think about shaving without getting hard now.

Alan guided Craig over to the chair. "Sit down, Little One."

Craig sat. His cock was so hard it strained upward and brushed against his stomach. Alan knelt in front of Craig. His gentle hands slid up Craig's calves and came to rest on the inside of his thighs. Slowly, he pushed Craig's legs apart.

"Hands behind your back, Little One."

Craig tucked his hands behind his back, then leaned back. He almost wished Alan had tied him up for this. Maybe next time, because there would be a next time.

Alan stood. Normally Craig barely noticed the difference in their height, but with Craig sitting and Alan looming over him, he looked so tall and imposing. Then he leaned down and pressed his lips against Craig's.

"Thank you, Sweetheart. This means a lot to me."

"You're welcome, Daddy. I love you."

"I love you, too." Alan's smile transformed from sweet, to sly. Craig's cock twitched in anticipation.

Craig watched Alan reach for the shaving cream. He squirted some into his hands and lathered it up a little.

"You can't wait, can you, Little One? You know this is going to feel amazing, don't you?"

"Yes, Daddy." Craig's voice was losing strength. All his focus was on Alan's hands.

"You can make as much noise as you want, Sweetheart, but you can't move. Especially once I get going with the razor. Daddy doesn't want to hurt you, so you need to stay really, really still. Can you do that for me?"

"Yes, Daddy." Craig's breathing was shallow.

"Good boy." Alan said as he reached down and lathered the base of Craig's cock with shaving cream. Craig's breathing hitched. The cream was cool on his skin and the way Alan touched him with such gentle adoration made Craig's insides melt.

"Look at you. So beautiful." Alan cooed as he gathered more shaving cream. Craig decided that Alan could shave Craig's entire body if he wanted to and Craig wouldn't care. The feel of Alan applying the shaving cream alone was worth it.

Then Alan grabbed the razor. Light glinted off the blade as Alan stroked his thumb across the blade to test for sharpness.

"Remember, Little One," Alan made eye contact with Craig. "You can't move at all. Not even a twitch."

"Yes, Daddy. I'll be still. I promise."

Alan knelt and got close. He wrapped the fingers of one hand around Craig's cock and held it out of the way while he made the first slow stroke of the razor. The sharp metal scraped Craig's skin smooth in one single stroke. Craig exhaled when Alan released his cock and reached over to rinse and dry the razor to prepare for the second pass.

"I told you that you'd look amazing like this. With your

pretty pink cock all hard for me." Alan made another pass with the razor and removed even more of Craig's dark hair. Craig couldn't find words to speak, he could barely remember to breathe.

"You're doing so good, being so still. If you keep it up, I'll definitely have to reward you." Alan kept talking, kept praising Craig as he dragged the razor down Craig's skin.

Craig watched the razor scrape another patch of flesh clean. Now all the hair that surrounded his cock was gone. Craig itched to reach down and feel the freshly shaven skin.

"Is it soft?" He asked.

Alan ran the tip of his finger along the naked skin. He hummed his approval. "Yes, Sweetheart. It's so soft. Imagine how soft the rest of you is going to be when I'm done."

"The rest of me?" Craig's breath caught in his throat.

Alan's smile was sweetly devious. "You didn't think I'd leave your nuts all fuzzy, did you? It's all got to come off."

Craig shifted a little. He wasn't exactly nervous. Alan did a great job so far, but the idea of someone having something that sharp that close to his nuts made him swallow.

"I think you're going to need to close your eyes for this, Little One." Alan said as he cleaned the razor off. "You're fidgeting."

"Sorry, Daddy." Craig took a breath and shut his eyes. It did help a little. He didn't have to watch the razor get closer to his skin. Craig forced himself to relax. Alan had never not looked after him.

Alan lifted his sack and shaved the back side first. Craig had never shaved himself there before. Once, he shaved the hair around his cock and it itched like a bitch when it grew back, so he didn't do it again. Shit. The itching. He'd forgotten about that.

A warm, wet cloth gently mopped the naked, and super sensitive skin. Alan's hands rested on the tops of Craig's thighs. Hot breath washed over the newly naked skin. Craig gasped at the foreign sensation. When warm, wet lips brushed against him, Craig's eyes popped open.

"God. Daddy. What're you doing?" Craig arched his back as Alan's tongue slicked around the base of Craig's naked cock. It was a sight to behold, though. Alan had been right about that. All the hair around his cock had been stripped away. He felt new and naked and really, really, dirty. "Fuck, that looks so good." Craig exhaled as Alan's tongue slid up the underside of Craig's shaft.

"I told you that you'd look amazing like this. All bare for me. You have such a pretty cock, Little One." Alan swirled his tongue around the head of Craig's cock. Then he dipped his head and went lower. Warm, wet heat enveloped Craig's nuts and he twitched. Everything was way more sensitive now.

"Fuck, that's good."

"I thought you'd like that." Alan grinned at him, then took Craig's cock in his mouth.

"Oh shit."

Alan sucked him all the way down, then pulled off. Craig's brain was fried. He let his head fall back and he stared at the ceiling.

"I'm going to be so itchy when it grows back."

Alan's fingers caressed the sensitive skin. Every muscle in Craig's body screamed as he fought to stay still.

"If I let it grow back."

Craig's head snapped up and he shot Alan a quizzical look.

"I think I like you like this, Sweetheart. Look at you. So pretty for Daddy."

"If you keep saying shit like that you can shave my whole body."

Alan stood up and held his hand out to Craig. "Come on, Little One. Daddy wants to do dirty things to that pretty cock of yours, but I'm getting too fucking old to kneel down for much longer."

Craig grinned and grabbed Alan's hand. "I think you should keep me like this." Craig said.

Alan cocked an eyebrow. "Yeah? You like it, do you?"

Craig ran a hand over the smooth skin. "I like it, but mostly I like that you like it." Craig wrapped his arms around Alan and pulled him into a kiss. "Now, about those dirty things you had planned for me."

The End

Acknowledgements

Here comes my favorite part of writing the book. The sappy 'I love you' portion where I get to tell the world what an awesome circle of friends I have. When I write I start with a scene and a book sort of unfolds from there. This book was no different. It started off with Craig walking into a kink club and being confronted with the fact that his former Dom is now a sub. *Surprise.* Of course… I'd never written a BDSM-ish book before (despite reading them by the truckload) and I'd written only a little MM romance. So color me nervous/terrified. I turned to Shaw Montgomery, who's a kink loving friend of mine, (go read her books, she's awesomesauce) and her encouragement and enthusiasm for Craig and Alan and their slightly unorthodox relationship really helped me get those first eight chapters out. I owe her one. Or two. Or ten.

Marie Namer swooped in one dark day and lit me up. She was kind and sweet and said things I needed to hear with absolute conviction and she made me believe that maybe I wasn't a total hack.

Parker Williams. Because Parker tried to distract me. But I'm undistracta—squirrel!

Courtney Bassett from LesCourt Author Services. I love you. You 'got' my book. You loved my boys as much as I did. You helped make them shine.

Kate Hawthorne. AKA MammaKink, thank you for letting me pick your brain.

The bestie gets absolutely no recognition whatsoever because he's been too busy to pay attention to me. So there.

About the Author

E. M. Denning is a married mom of three and a writer from British Columbia. She loves her family and her animals and anything cute and fuzzy. She writes romance for the 18+ crowd because she is both a hopeless romantic and a dirty old woman.

Follow her on Facebook: facebook.com/emdenning
Subscribe to her newsletter!
Join her exclusive Facebook group: Denning's Darlings!

Made in the USA
Columbia, SC
08 September 2018